# Drum Roll

by
Anne T. Billson

authorHOUSE™

1663 LIBERTY DRIVE, SUITE 200
BLOOMINGTON, INDIANA 47403
(800) 839-8640
WWW.AUTHORHOUSE.COM

*First published by AuthorHouse 10/31/05*

*ISBN: 1-4208-8458-1 (sc)*

*Printed in the United States of America
Bloomington, Indiana*

*This book is printed on acid-free paper.*

## ACKNOWLEDGEMENTS

All characters in this novel are fictitious, and any resemblance to living persons, present or past, is coincidental.

# PROLOGUE

The two-note sound of the chains pulled at me in the early afternoon air. It worried me like the whine of a child, frightened of being left alone and deserted. I moved to the bottom step of the back porch. A slight wind came up and the trees rustled. "Don't," I told them, "Don't say anything more. It's done."

Nothing can live without something dying. I knew how the pharoahs must have felt when they saw the last stone being placed on a pyramid. The oaks was the story of my life.

# CHAPTER 1

The Hynm "Rock of Ages" fell from the choir loft of Saint Matthew's Episcopal Church in Macon, Georgia. The singing gripped my throat and caused tears to pour down my face. I was twelve years old and silent grief was permissible. My mother sat next to me in the Worthington pew swathed like a black cocoon alongside my older sister and brother. My father lay in a dark gray closed coffin, smothered, as were the aisles, nave, and even the chior loft, by a glut of suffocating flowers. The congregation appeared to be suspended in genuine sorrow, probably in terror for their own mortality and shock. Disbelief. I heard someone say later, "Sam was so young, not even forty, kind and generous. Everyone loved him. There was no way he could have survived his bout with pneumonia; poor Eugenia and the children."

Outside, on the green lawns of College Street, and across to the opposite curbstone, stood dozens of blacks whose champion my father had been. I saw them standing in the sun through the stained glass windows opened to mid-afternoon June air. A low persistent hum rose from the mass of humanity. It was a strange one or two key harmonized moan that came from them as they swayed back and forth, side to side.

I watched The minister step forward of the pulpit to speak.

"He's an old shit," my brother Emory said.

My mother's face, surrounded by folds of black tulle remained impassive. Miss Eugenie was beautiful, tall and regal with a slow grace of movement.

After my father's death, sociability still flickered in my mother. She chose to live behind an invisible wall where she felt protected from the cruelty of time and its changes. I often watched as she roamed around her flower garden, humming, played the piano, and read her books. Her supper conversation was filled with quotations of her favorites, the English Romantics.

"Strangeness is their dominant element," she told us. "Realism is abhorrent to them."

Claudia, my older sister, leaned her head back and stared at the ceiling. Emory looked at the wine cruet without blinking his dark eyes until he was offered another "sip". After supper he went to the stall of his horse, Thunderclap, and I heard them pounding down the driveway toward Vineville Avenue, without caring about the traffic, or the men going home after work to happy families.

While in the kitchen two weeks after my father was buried, I asked Dola, "Where does Emory go?" She turned around at the sink and scowled. "Being nosy killed a cat. How come you ask so many questions?"

"Well, he is my brother and I really don't know him at all. He's never at home much."

"And you is complaining 'bout that?"

"Where does he go and what does he do?"

3

She scowled again, "Ask him."

"I'm scared of Emory. Besides, I'm not sure he knows I'm alive."

"Count your blessings."

Dola was always allowed to speak her mind because no other person in Macon except Maybelle, a black teenager and another of our servants, would work in the house with my brother Emory. In spite of his wild reputation all over middle Georgia, he remained forever first in our mother's affections.

"The day he was born he was already twenty years old," Claudia told me more than once. "He went from mothers' milk to bourbon. We all had wet nurses, you know. The woman who fed him must have been delivered to the back door by Daddy's bootlegger."

Years later, I was still afraid of Thunderclap with his rolling eyeballs and high-pitched whinnies. When his stomping and jerking against the bit got out of control in the small paddock back of our old playhouse, Willie Fosters, the part-time groom, touched him with the flat of his hand and spoke low against his neck. Thunderclap settled down to pawing sparse grass and dipped his head toward the red dirt. My brown eyes met Willie's blue ones through the wood-slat fence of the paddock and I was unable to speak. When I turned away my throat closed and I was unable to swallow.

Over racing heartbeats I heard gentled notes from Miss Eugenie's piano. At nightfall her music was soft and wistful like a wave of her hand to the last of daylight, a farewell murmur to familiar, shared sights until she faced the dark alone.

I wondered what she was like as a wife.

Our Daddy flew to Argentina every few years to buy different types of leather goods for his chain of department stores in the South. The lightness of our lives left with him and Miss Eugenie's migraines began. Claudia never told me why she always cried before his departures. Our father's homecomings were carnivals of presents and stories. Once he brought back a black carp in a container of water for the fishpond.

I wish I could say more about my father. Memories of him come in smallness; the way an oak branch moves in a slight breath of air, pushing aside a leaf or two that block a moment's glimpse of brightness. Suddenly there is the back of his head with dark hair. Or I remember Claudia and Emory running to a window on a late afternoon when his car drove down the driveway, calling out, "He's home!"

"Let's mix them up," Daddy had said, "see if the other carp make this black fellow go to the back of the pool. See if he can swim as well as they do. Let's see if the color of skin really matters worth a damn anyhow."

Each time he returned from a trip, I hoped my Daddy had found more in South America than a black carp and leather goods. I hoped he found a Dolores, no, not that name; it means sorrow or pain, but maybe a Margarita. Margarita is a name with a rhythm to it like two hands stroking a drum. Maybe he would find a Margarita who did the flamenco for him with castanets clattering back and forth as her bare cocoa body gleamed in lamplight. I wanted him to have had that, but I didn't think he

6

did. Dola had said, while Claudia nodded her head, that Daddy loved Miss Eugenie.

As Claudia entered the kitchen one morning, she kept flicking ashes onto the floor. "Emory has been a bastard again," she said.

"So what else is new," Dola shot back, "and clean up those ashes."

Claudia ignored Dola's request and continued. "Would you believe the day Emory was born he was already twenty years old? He went from mothers' milk to bourbon. Each of us had wet nurses, you know. The woman that fed him must have been delivered to the back door by Daddy's bootlegger."

"I've heard you tell that story a dozen times," I said. But I wondered why we had wet nurses.

My mother was intensely private with us. When her bedroom door opened in the morning she was completely dressed including stockings and pumps of soft fine leather. In my now eighteen years I'd never seen her in a state of partial undress or with a strand of brown hair escaping the figure eight twisted against the back of her long slender neck. She wore only a sprinkling of powder and a light touch of rouge on her pale face. My mother was remote from us; perhaps she was there for him. They must have had something together or she would not have grieved so long. It was six years after his death and she still wore black dresses from September to March, then pale lavender or pastels through spring and summer.

Whenever I walked into the house from my classes at St. Joseph's Academy and saw Mother playing the piano in a light-colored dress my heart leapt. The golden mist, an imperceptible haze that began in late February and hung over honeysuckle vines, had settled into tiny buds that could open at any hour and cause me to wait with unmoving beneath the trellises on our back lawn. Wisteria and roses would soon fill bleak spaces of winter and I found myself reaching for something unknowable as I stood at another beginning. Years ago our house was surrounded by many large oak trees. I remember pretending I was a wood nymph under a sky of green lace. After the death of my father, Miss Eugenie had three of the largest and most beautiful ones cut down."Germs flourish in so much shade," she said to me. "Did you know that sunshine is God's greatest cure-all?"

I still miss the three old friends with lichen moss on their gray trunks whose swirls and furrows were known to my eyes and fingers since I was able to walk. As I grew older, I wondered why they were destroyed because they would have helped my mother stay alone and hidden from the outside world.

Each time Dola answered the front door, she knew to say, Miss Eugenie is resting now," or, "Ain't nobody to home. Just leave your calling card please, ma'am."

Years of this charade turned the world of Macon, Georgia, from our door except for Miss Agatha Hollingsworth. Miss Agatha, tall and lean as a whooping crane, had been Miss Eugenie"s roommate at Gunston Hall and later her maid of honor. Miss Haggie, as my sister called her, paid no attention to Dola and shouted through the open door, "Stop this nonsense, Eugenie. I know you're in there somewhere and I'm coming in to see you."

My mother would rise like a swan from a deep chair where she hid from intruders and floated toward the front door. "Why, Aggie, what a pleasant surprise!" This scene was played time after time without the change of dialouge or different tone in the voices.

The only other friends allowed to visit The Oaks were the Episcopal minister Charles Culpepper and his wife, Miss Suzannah. Even Dola could not look into their gracious faces and tell a lie.

Miss Eugenie would place a slender hand at her throat and finger her single strand of pearls. "They are American royalty," she'd say each time they visited. I'm related to each of them on my mother's side. He is my grandfather's --- the linage became involved and difficult for her and led to another worthy line on her father's side. Cluadia closed her eyes and looked asleep. I tuned Miss Eugenie out to a lilting murmur in the background like honeybees hovering over one of her rose beds.

Dola wrinkled her forehead. "Oh, Jesus, I'm glad I knows nothing 'bout my old folks way back. All I know is they are colored and they was damn fools."

Sometimes I lay on my back with my dog Fellow in the Greenery under an ancient oak our mother had spared. It was covered by kudzu vines. Fellow's head lay on my shoulder while he snored in dog snorts and I thought about that. My mother had God, Emory, and Claudia. Dola had hidden lovers in the cellar, lying on their sides in the wine racks waiting for an eager touch, but I had Fellow, and the Greenery was our secret place. I stared up into leaves of the kudzu vines that pulsed as they stretched inch by inch for new life.

Our regular yard man kept the vines under control when my Daddy was alive. Now they ran wild, covered the stone wall bordering one side of our property and feathering out to overcome two large oak trees in the right hand corner of our huge yard.

"Stop them," my mother called out to Joe Henry, "their leafy ropes grow twelve inches overnight. Someday we'll wake up and find ourselves entombed by those vines."

The Greenery was beautiful to us, me and Fellow. Occasionally while reading in its shade I'd look out at the old fishpond and any sadness I felt would disappear. Sometimes I reminisced about how we once sat upon flat stones around it to feed the carp that gathered at sunset. In spring water lily pads had grown as large as dinner plates; whoever happened to be with me watched fish wander and flash among them. The pond had been a source of pride to Miss Eugenie; also the camellia bushes she tended near the front gate. Every friend that came to visit remarked on the beauty of the blooms and glossy leaves. The bushes still thrived luxuriously although the fishpond was now an empty relic. Rain left a few inches of dirty water on the bottom and once in awhile Fellow barked defiantly at a frog that sat on the cement slopes. It was obvious the frog resented any intrusion near his resting place near the large green cocoon that he may have felt belonged to him and the kudzu vines.

# CHAPTER 2

Claudia's silences became longer and more frequent as she lay on one of the living room sofas staring at the chandelier. She held a cigarette in her fingers while the ash grew. It was hypnotic to watch and I wondered when the gray cone would give in to the laws of gravity.

"It's not ladylike to lie on the couch like that," Miss Eugenie said. "I suggest you sit upright with your spine against the back of the couch."

Claudia's green gaze swung toward her. "I'm not a lady."

"That's absurd," our mother said.

Claudia kicked her legs in the air and laughed. "Watch this." She blew a wobbly smoke ring into the air.

Miss Eugenie walked away. "I've never seen anything so unfeminine in my whole life."

I grabbed Dola's hand as she waved a dust rag over an end table. "What talent she has," I said. "When my mother leaves, a room becomes bereft. Only stick furniture and paper doll people are left."


"Miss Eugenie sho can pull the blinds down easy like when she don't want to see nothing," Dola said.

Later Miss Eugenie came in with camellia stems covered with dark leaves and pale buds spilling from her arms. "These are so lovely, Cady. Why don't you take them over to Miss Pridey's with some of Dola's bread? Maybe Claudia would like to go with you?"

My sister shrugged and rose from the sofa in graceful slow motion. We walked together to our next-door neighbor's two-story red brick house. Miss Pridey was a recluse. Four once-white columns across the front porch had not been repainted in my lifetime, had peeled off to show big patches of gray plaster.

"If she's not at home we can leave these flowers with Zeldee, the cook," I said.

Claudia began to laugh. "Not at home?". I put my hand on her arm to restrain her. "Miss Pridey hasn't been beyond her front gate in twenty years," she said.

Zeldee answered the resounding noise created by the heavy brass knocker on the front door and took our gifts. "Miss Pridey ain't well."

Behind her we saw a bleached blonde head with splotches on her face peer from the stairwell. "Hey Miss Pridey" I yelled through the crack in the door. "How you?" I waved. No answer.

I took Claudia's arm to lead her back toward the front steps.

"I worry about Miss Pridey," I said. "She's so thin and frail. It's just not normal to act the way she does."

I let her go into her wild laughter undisturbed. "What is normal?" Claudia asked. On Vineville Avenue she stopped and leaned back against a telephone pole with her eyes closed. "Pain and darkness," she said quietly. "Knowledge and silence."

I pulled at her arm. "We're almost home."

With her eyes still shut, she said, "Whee."

15

Miss Eugenie was humming as she walked around her flower garden on the back lawn. "How is Miss Pridey?"

Claudia drifted into a chair by degrees like a fragile puppet. "The news is bad. She's exactly the same."

"How is her skin allergy?"

"From the small part of her face that we saw, I would say she appears to be a walking pimple."

"That's unkind," our mother said.

Claudia's skin had the texture and sheen of a camellia bloom in July. Her appearance was startling with her high cheekbones and crow-black hair hanging loose on her shoulders. When I looked into her eyes before she turned away, I saw a green flame with an intensity that frightened me.

Later I saw Claudia watching Willie Fosters work while we sat on the backyard swing before supper. He had worked for us for five years taking care of Emory's horse. Willie lived with his parents in one of the identical two-room frame houses beyond the high steel fence that separated our neighborhood from the cotton mill. As he moved across the back lawn turning soil with a spade for an autumn flower garden, Claudia's face followed him like a shadow on a sundial. His brown hair had lightened from summer's sun, seemed to pale his eyes startlingly blue. Willie was the same age as our brother Emory, two years older than Claudia. I worried about that. At twenty she was beautiful. She sat on the back lawn swing pretending to read. I leaned toward her looking through my eye-slits while she lifted her glance from a magazine and followed every move of Willie's tall lanky body. Miss Eugenie asked me about my homework, then went into the house. Hidden from anyone else's sight, Willie's eyes met mine. He gave me a gentle smile before he moved behind one of the huge oak trees. After supper I brought a few sugar cubes to Emory's horse Thunderclap. Willie leaned against the back wall of our old playhouse and watched me feed him. Our silences together that summer hung in the air, rich and heavy with messages we could not shape into words. The sun dropped behind the chinaberry tree in the far corner of the back fence and shot colors at us through the branches. My eyes held onto Willie's face like someone who is lost at sea and looks with longing for the reassurance of the North Star.

A mild breeze lifted his light-brown hair. I wanted to know what would lessen the distance between us. Which of the identical white box houses of the mill workers did he live in with his parents? On hot summer nights did he strip and go swimming in the millpond a half-mile away in a patch of pine woods? In my mind I saw him standing tall on the bank where the stream widened, his flanks taunt, stomach flat, his beautifully shapely back tensed for a dive through darkness into darker water.

Now when our eyes held, I leaned against the back of the swing and my breathing changed.

Willie was due to leave in November for Army basic training in North Carolina. I knew I was in love; wondered how my days could go on without seeing him. Curled up later on the window seat upstairs with an ache in my stomach, I saw Claudia in her doorway watching me. When she went into her room, I sneaked out the back door.

Willie cleaned his gardening tools, then hung them on the outside wall of my old playhouse. We looked at each other in short quick glances. My feelings made me tremble and I turned my head away.

"I'll take care of our garden while you're gone, Willie," I managed to say.

We sat apart on the back lawn swing, hidden from the house by the porch railing covered with wisteria vines. Each of us leaned against opposite ends until the feelings became too intense. Our fingers moved together and clung. I looked at the anguish in his eyes.

"Have you seen my place in the Greenery?" I asked. He didn't answer. In one move we rose together and walked into the tangled mass that spread above us. Remnants of dying kudzu hung from lower branches of the old oaks. We sat on earth that smelled of growth and death, all the cycles of life that continued in this place. I was conscious of the curve of his thigh, the beauty of his rough, tanned hands, and I barely breathed. He turned me around and brought my face toward him, then lowered his mouth carefully, slowly onto mine.

When he pulled away, Willie placed his head in a cupped hand supported by his elbow and looked into my

19

eyes. "Do you remember the story about Fine Pup I told you seems like years ago."

I saw sadness in his eyes as he blinked tears. "Not really--tell me again."

"It's sad," he said, "Don't know why this place reminds me of him; maybe it's because of the love the master and dog had for one another—like you and Fellow. Miss Lily, the lady the black man Dawson worked for, allowed him to bring his dog Fine Pup to work if he tied him to her plum tree."

"What's the sense of keeping these flower beds so nice if Fine Pup digs every which way," she had said.

"She remembered the morning the dog had torn down all the wisteria and lit into her rose bushes," Willie said. "Dawson remembered. Evidently Fine Pup was feeling the sweetness of life and had run round and round the back garden. From that day on Fine Pup, a good sized dog now, stayed at the end of a rope somewhere near him. Dawson told me he explained everything he was doing to the dog, who, once in awhile, thumped his tail to show he was listening. When the sun moved down toward Miss Lily's back wall and the smoke stack of the cotton mill blew sharp as a gun blast, Dawson would untie the rope, knock on the back door to lift his hat to Miss Lily before setting out for home. A mile away, both he and Fine Pup knew when to cross the street to the other side and when to cross back again. Houses became smaller; they were white framed boxes with A-model Fords parked in front. One or two people sat on porches in rocking chairs or on an old wooden swing. Creaking of the chains stopped and the swings sat still when Dawson and Fine Pup walked by. He told me he would lift his hat to the folks and bowed a little but silence came from the porches; thick and heavy as Georgia deep water clouds."

Willie stopped a moment, wet his finger and traced my mouth. "Want me to go on? Things get worse."

I nodded.

"Dawson told me he dreaded the next block. The mill hands would shout, 'Shffle them feet, boy,' or call out 'Hurry along now. We don't want any negras moving 'bout round here after sundown.'"

"'Although I have grey hair, I'll have to answer to 'boy' the rest of my life,' he confided in me once then said,

'Fine Pup always dances on his hind legs when we would reach Pleasant Hill for Colored Folks. It was Home-time, supper-time, then snuggling-in-bed-time. While we snuggled, I was able to look at whatever picture books the mailman had brought that day. Wondrous things, full of color and shine, like red wagons for children or fine blue coats and pants to match for menfolk. The ladies in their different colored dresses were like angles must be.' It was then that he asked me if his deceased wife Ella was a white angel now. And were there ever any brown ones? 'I don't think so,' he'd say. 'All the church windows I've washed in Macon have white angels with yellow hair hanging to their shoulders. My Ella has been gone twelve years now; Miss Lily paid for everything after Ella died in childbirth; the birthing lady could not turn our breached child. It was after both deaths that she gave me Fine Pup to keep me company.'"

Willie hesitated, leaned down to kiss me lightly again.

I pushed him away. "Finish. And don't leave anything out."

"As Dawson talked, he waved his hat before his face to cool sweat trickling in rivlets down his forehead and into his eyes. 'Miss Lily always handed me ice tea on a hot day like today and would say, Rest now, a little, in the shade. It was on such a day that I fell into a doze and woke to long shadows, and, in my hand an empty rope loop. I looked under every bush, every nook where Fine Pup may have hidden. Nothing. My breath stopped. Fine Pup was a man-dog now, not a pup and a tease. My heart filled my throat when I knocked on Miss Lily's door and told her I had to leave. He's chasing some lady dog most likely,' he said to her."

"The story has it that Miss Lily warned Dawson to stay away from the mill people. 'I'm scared of those folks,' she said, 'they're mean as snakes to the blacks, so stay away, you hear?'"

"The rest is heresy, but I'll tell it to you anyway. Dawson walked around the block, then ran the mile to the mill grounds looking everywhere, he passed smells of collard greens cooking and raw gray dirt without a blade of grass anywhere to a group of men standing by the mill pond. 'Sir,' he said to one of them. 'My black and white dog is missing. He's 'bout so high.'"

"The men laughed. 'No, he ain't missing,' one said. 'He just turned into a fish, is all. He's at the bottom of that there mill pond. Been there for nigh on a half hour. We weighted him down with stones. He was so dumb he just stood still, thought we was playing a game with him 'til the big heave-to and the splash.'"

"Dawson didn't look at the mill pond. His eyes held those of the white man without a move as tears slid down his face, his chin, wetting his shirt and slid into his hands. He stared at the men, then bent to lay his hat on red dirt. In one leap, he cleared the bank and sank in murky water. It was certain he was looking for Fine Pup, but only felt broken beer bottles and bottom sand. It is said that he, too, drowned looking for his dog. The mill hands got off scott free."

Willie bent over to look into my eyes. My tear ducts were working overtime. He kissed my closed eyelids and said, "That's a true story; I didn't mean to make you sad; just wanted to tell you a story about a man's love for his dog; like your love for Fellow. I grabbed him around the neck and held him to me.

I heard Dola call for me to come inside before dark. We walked out of the Greenery afraid to touch each other. The last light of afternoon sun slid past the far eves of the house and flung its spectrum of colors from behind the chinaberry tree toward the Greenery.

"You're still crying, Cady."

"I'm not, Willie." I lied. "I'm not crying at all." I turned my head to hide the rush of tears on my face.

I leaned on an elbow and called to the black man who bent over my bedroom fireplace in the hint of light before dawn. "Joe Henry, what time is it?"

"Ain't no call for you to be stirring 'bout. Won't be sun-up for a while yet." He clumped away to light fires in other rooms both upstairs and down before the ladies of the house awoke.

I dressed by firelight. In another week we would need furnace heat in the early mornings. In another month Willie would be gone, the playhouse empty and also me.

I found him in the spreading glow of the sun, stroking Thunderclap.

"Cady, you'll have to take good care of yourself when I leave, you hear? Dola will help you."

He held my head against his chest before he kissed me.

# CHAPTER 3

Miss Eugenie insisted and almost forced me to date boys she chose. Her favorite was Berkley Hollingworth, the only child of her best friend Miss Aggie. Up north all winter at another college, he had made it through the whole year before he was requested not to return because of "insubordinate behavior."

Berkley knew I took summer courses at Mercer University and always called in the middle of the afternoon to speak to Miss Eugenie before I arrived home from Spanish class. I imagined my mother slipping into her Southern Belle manner and cooing into the phone; it wasn't an affectation but a second skin that fell over her during any contact with the male sex.

Mother's ability to speak in a lilting girlish voice and glare at me with cold threatening eyes at the same time amazed me.

"How sweet of you to think of us. Cady is walking in right now but let me take the message while she puts her books away."

Berkley probably told her of a movie or some plan he had made for the next Saturday night. Miss Eugenie accepted with, "It all sounds thrilling, and of course, Cady would be delighted to go."

"I refuse," I called out in a loud voice. "You know I hate and despise Berkley Hollingsworth."

Mother's voice curtsied goodbye and she hung up. "Don't be ridiculous, Cady." The Southern Belle manner slid off her like a snake's skin in summer. "His great-grandfather was in President Davis' cabinet. His family has been close to mine for generations."

"I will not go out with him."

"He's a flower of Southern manhood and of course you're going. I've given my word." She turned away.

I dreaded any date with Berkley. At the end of the evening I jumped out of his car when he slowed to almost a stop when he turned into our driveway. Berkley was a biter; on the rare occasions that he trapped me after he bruised my mouth with his teeth, he lowered his head and tried to bite my breasts. I risked a broken ankle by leaping out of the car but it was better than fighting his sharp little nips.

Dates with Berkley never varied.

"When we're married," he would begin, "we'll go to New York on our honeymoon. I know the city well."

"Don't make any plans, Berkley," I'd say.

"You're going to marry me, sugar-tit," he said.

"Really? Where are we going tonight?"

"To bed."

"I've already seen the movie you suggested, but let's go again—anything is better than riding around with you."

"We're not going to be riding around. We are going to be galloping away in a horizontal position."

"Either we go to a movie or I will get out of this car at the next stop light."

After the movie and as we drove down Vineville Avenue toward my home, he said, "You'll be much nicer when you lose your virginity. It'll sweeten you up."

"That's something you will never know," I said. When he slowed to a stop to turn into our gate, I leapt from the car.

"Don't forget the Friday night dance at the Club," he called out.

"I have other plans."

"Eight o'clock," he leaned his head out of the window. "Don't be late as you usually are."

Sometimes during the next few days, Berkley lost the use of his family's car due to drunken behavior in public. A taxi drove up to our house at eight o'clock on Friday night. Men in uniform appeared in town now and we all felt suspended in the quickened air of a country at war again. To save gas, I think the taxis doubled up fares. This one had two strangers waiting inside. Berkley pulled me onto his lap. Within two blocks I felt hardness beneath me and turned to glare at him. He began making up and down moves that even I understood.

"Are you crazy?" I hissed at him.

The soldier seated next to us laughed low in his throat as he tilted his head back to take a swig from a bottle he carried in a paper bag.

Sexual play going on in a crowded taxi? Even for Berkley that was unbelievable. "Stop the car, please," I asked the driver.

Berkley's arm tightened around my waist. "Keep going."

"Help me," I called out." From the far corner of the seat I heard the unmistakable accent of Southern mountain country.

He leaned forward and said in a deep voice, "Leave the poor girl be."

I nodded my thanks to him. I didn't want tears in my voice to show.

Willie, Willie, where are you?

# CHAPTER 4

October had floated past in yellow air; November was naked reality. Trees shivered their few die-hard brown leaves. My mother complained again about Fellow coming into the house at night to sleep.

"What about Thunderclap?" she asked me. "Do you want him to come inside, too, just because the weather is a little nippy?"

"Thunderclap too mean to freeze," Dola said. "He got the fires of Hell burning in his insides anyways. I can tell by them rolling eyeballs."

"Please, Mother," I begged her.

"I'll think about it." That meant "yes" and I was almost happy.

Fellow was my best friend and slept under the covers with his feathery Collie tail on the other pillow beside me. I wanted to ask some of the out-of-town girls at Mercer to spend a weekend with me but I could not bear having them go back to the dormitory and tell stories about my family. Sometimes I felt we had halted in time--or worse, that time had stopped for us.

Most of my local friends had drifted away because of Emory's reputation. He was arrested last year for being drunk and disorderly in GLORIA'S NIGHTCLUB in downtown Macon.

"I was friends with your daddy, son, and your granddaddy," the Judge said when Emory stood before the bench. "Now get out of here and don't let me see you again."

He was back numerous times to stand before different faces to hear the same words.

I knew this tore at Miss Eugenie's soul but she never mentioned it. Before death, before sickness or poverty, the worst calamity that could strike us was disgrace. Scandal gnawed at the roots of our Deep Southern existence.

Swaddling clothes that had protected our lives since birth were held by the web of silence we hid in. No one was allowed across this tangled space.

There was no password for entrance into our seclusion.


Before Christmas, Thursday became Miss Eugenie's war effort night at Camp Wheeler. Once a week she took a deep satchel and drove with it out through pine woods to the Infantry Training Camp on the outskirts of Macon to spend two hours teaching a class of eighteen year old inductees to read and write. They came from several Southern states and each one loved Miss Eugenie. On military paydays she brought home two large paper bags filled with presents they bought for her at the PX; candy bars, white silk scarves with "America the Beautiful" printed on them, beer mugs shaped like a charging infantryman, once a Statue of Liberty lamp, and always one or two bottles of Delight Tonight perfume. She showed each gift to us with pride, then put them back in the paper bags for Dola and Maybelle to divide between themselves and take home.

"That's a big mistake," Claudia said the first time. "Dola will probably drink the perfume and the kitchen will smell like an orange grove for a week."

Miss Eugenie's stare directed to her was a sudden glimpse of a far-off frozen sea. Even Claudia lowered her eyes before it.

Emory wrote from a flight School in Athens and came home for a weekend each month, long enough for the fluttering Miss Eugenie to insist that Dola use most of our ration coupons on feasts for him. Once he brought a photo of himself standing by the side of a pretty girl with a pine tree behind them. She looked up at him as he scowled at the camera. My classmates at school told me he was extremely handsome when I showed them the snapshot. I tried to look at the picture objectively--he was too brooding. He should have been rushing across an English moor wearing a cape against the wind.

I was alone except for my Fellow. I passed the closed door of my mother's room and knew she was kneeling on her prie-dieu praying for Emory's safety. Claudia withdrew more than ever. She lay on a couch with her eyes closed most of the day. Miss Eugenie stopped suggesting that the two of us go to a movie, the library, the Country Club swimming pool or tennis courts.

I stared at the windows and watched the oaks fight northern winds. They flailed their branches wildly, declaring their turf with solid trunks held steady against autumn gusts. I turned to Claudia who appeared to be asleep.

"Berkley Hollingsworth will be home soon for the holidays. He's often said you are beautiful and exotic-looking, and he's only about a year or two younger than you."

"I don't need your cast-offs," her eyes stayed closed. "Any of them."

After a while I said, "We could play double solitaire or honeymoon bridge."

"We could also hush talking and let me have a little peace."

"What can I do," I asked Dola in the kitchen. "There must be a way to reach her, get her interested in something."

"Baby, quit trying to change this old world. Best be happy in your own little piece of it and let the rest float by."

I thought a minute. "But that's selfish."

"No, it ain't. It's looking the truth in the face and saying 'Hoo! You don't scare <u>me</u> none. That's what I want to see you doing, you hear me talking?"

# CHAPTER 5

Berkley arrived the day before Thanksgiving. Another Connecticut prep school had been amenable to a new stained glass window in the chapel and accepted him as a student. He greeted us the first night home with the same arrogance on his chiseled features, but a smooth veneer had settled upon him, an urbanity rare among our local boys. He talked to Miss Eugenie about the war in Iraq and Afghanistan; our expected progress in each country, terrorism, and the Al-Qaeda. My mother's eyes glowed as he reminded her of the American fighting spirit. Her forebears had fought in every war for our country since its beginning and she listened raptly, blue eyes shining, hands clasped in her lap. When the clock struck nine, she excused herself and climbed the stairs.

We heard her bedroom door close and I felt myself pushed backward on the couch with Berkley pinning me down by lying on top of me, his tongue trying to force my lips apart to reach deep into my throat. I rolled from beneath him, sat on the floor and looked up at him.

"You phoney son of a bitch! I thought you had grown up a little. You haven't changed one single bit."

"Well, you certainly have," he said. "Your hair looks a lot blonder. If you're putting peroxide on it in secret, keep it up. You look like a two-eyed Veronica Lake and you're filling out nicely. Your breasts are as good as any I've seen in the North."

"All that talk to my mother about the war and our country! I'll set her straight tomorrow about your true character. Count on it."

"Cady, Cady, don't fight it." He knelt beside me on the rug and grabbed my hands. "I'm going to take you now across a new threshold and show you wonders you've never dreamed of."

I pulled my hands away. "If you show me one thing, Berkley, I'll scream at the top of my voice. And if my mother doesn't believe me, Willie Fosters will when he comes home on furlough. He'll find you wherever you are."

"So it's you and the mill boy now." He leaned back on his heels. "That's really tacky, Cady. Shameful."

"Please go, Berkley. We have nothing more to say to each other." I walked to the front door and held it open.

"You have a great little ass," he said while close behind me.

"Goodnight, Berkley," I dodged his outstretched arms, then pushed him through the door and slammed it. Safe, I ran up the stairs.

On Christmas Eve I asked Miss Eugenie to please telephone Mr. McMartin, the owner of the cotton mill who lived across the street from us, and ask him in which of the white box houses Willie's parents lived.

"I would like to call on them, maybe take them a bottle of one of our wines for Christmas," I explained.

Miss Eugenie savored her mid-morning coffee in the breakfast room; the apple-green table and walls contrasted with the grayness of our back lawn through the windows behind her. Twisted wisteria vines on trellises looked barren and dead.

She turned her head toward the door into the kitchen and raised her voice. "Dola, please give me a list of anything you need from the grocery store. I'm going to call in our order now."

When she turned back to me the blankness in her eyes erased my words as if they were dead leaves rushing by in a sudden gust of winter wind.

Willie sent me a Christmas card with a collie dog in a Santa Claus cap on the front. Inside he wrote: "Fellow had better be taking good care of you all. Been promoted to sargent. Only have one picture of you and most of that is Thunderclap. How about one with just your face and your yellow hair to keep with me all the time. Hope I'll be home sometime in May."

"You done wore out that card from Willie Fosters, sleeping with it under your pillow," Dola told me in early January.

"How do you know it's from Willie?" I said. "I would not dream of reading other people's mail."

"Hoo!" she said. "Don't act no high and mighty with me. I got enough of that 'round here."

Spring was sudden. One day the warmth of late March surrounded us and new life was everywhere. Especially in me. Kudzu vines turned green and tiny tendrils curled along branches of the oaks--hesitant, feathery beginnings that would soon rush forth, eager and free.

I hung a large calendar inside my closet door. Underneath the bold words LOY WILKINS LUMBER YARD were X's where I marked off the days until May. Hidden from Claudia's and Miss Eugenie's eyes, I stared at it and touched the numbers in each square with my fingers.

I felt stirring in every part of the yard. The dogwood tree by the driveway shouted up at me one morning when I went to the window and saw it covered with flat white blooms.

I ran to another window. Will you hide us again soon, my beautiful, beautiful kudzu vines?

# CHAPTER 6

Dola told me everyday to stand up straight and stop moping around.

"What you got to fret about? Willie Fosters done come home and gone again and don't think I ain't such a prize fool I don't see what going on twixt you two."

"Nothing's going on between us, if you please. And kindly don't talk about it," I begged her. "It's hard enough to get through the day trying not to think of how much I miss him."

"Jesus, on top of all my other troubles now I got somebody lovesick on my hands who don't know when she be lucky."

"Lucky? Pray tell me how I'm lucky."

"Just take my word. I knows more than anybody in this crazy house ever dream of. And you is lucky."

"Please share your wisdom with me, oh, great one."

"Go 'long with you. I ain't got time for no more drooping ladies. This place go to hell and back if'n I was to lean a little myself."

My memories fed me like the heaviest of thick sweet cream. I leaned against a door jamb, a chair, the wall by the staircase and the throat-closing flood overtook me and left me limp. Willie had asked me to wait for him--a good choice of words, "wait". I wanted to run to him pellmell, over any hurdles, any time.

The Oaks changed even more. Eula Belle was now in nursing school; Joe Henry worked at the defense plant south of Macon, a sitting-down job he assured Miss Eugenie when he came by for his Sunday dinner. Maybelle married an Alabama boy who was overseas. She stopped by for a few hours each day to help Dola. The late-stage of her pregnancy made us all nervous.

"I assume you know something about childbirth," Claudia asked Dola one afternoon while a long strange look held their eyes together.

"Enough," Dola finally answered. "I knows how they gets in and I knows how they gets out."

Claudia's beauty held my eyes with her black hair thick and long against her shoulders and her skin whiter than ever. Mother tried to tempt her to eat more, but she lived on the late summer air alone.

"If your appetite doesn't improve, I'm going to insist that you see Dr. Parker. You're much too thin."

"Insist all you like. I'm not going anywhere."

"Our cousins in Richmond have many young people your age around all the time", she said. "Why don't you think about visiting them before summer is over?"

"Is it summer? I hadn't noticed."

I knew that was not true. When Willie had come home on furlough she wore revealing dresses, low-cut on top, with thin swirling skirts clinging to her long legs. She sat on the back lawn swing watching him as he worked for hours each day trying to hold back the heavy touches of time on our shrubbery and repair its damage to the house.

Miss Eugenie insisted I continue my full-time classes at Mercer and I knew Claudia was alone with Willie, hidden from my mother's eyes by rich late spring growth. I didn't make good grades that semester.

Dog days came in the middle of August. Fellow slept most of the day at the back door and roused only to thump his tail against the porch when I passed him or leaned down to kiss the top of his head.

Miss Eugenie stayed in her room reading books or writing to Emory at her rosewood desk. His frequent letters home asked questions about each of us.

"It takes a war to make one aware of how deep his roots really are," Miss Eugenie said after she finished reading one of his letters aloud to us as we sat on the back porch watching lawn sprinklers try to swish life into browning grass.

Claudia listened with her green eyes closed.

"There is just nothing we can do but commend him to God's care." Our mother folded the white sheets of paper and pressed them against her chest.

"You do that," Claudia mumbled, half asleep.

The heavy air affected each of us. Miss Eugenie no longer stroked her Chopin etudes, but stretched Wagner and Beethoven to an emotional, pounding breaking point. Passion hurling from the keyboard left us drained when at last silence settled among us like the eye of a storm.

I slept poorly. Willie explained why he wrote fewer letters. He had another promotion, and training his men in gunnery practice filled his days. Gentle Willie who soothed the wildness in Thunderclap by the lightest touch was teaching young men how to kill.

"I have to give each one the best possible chance for survival," he wrote. "Some of these guys who came in as kids must learn to be tough. This war is ugly. When I go to my sack each night I think of you, little Cady. This unwanted war makes me want to learn everything it takes to just stay alive."

I read the first part aloud to Dola in the breakfast room and saw Claudia listening behind the half-closed door.

That night I reached under my pillow to stroke his letter but it was gone.

I awoke to choking heat. "No breakfast, please," I told Dola.

My Spanish class let out early because black clouds piled up in the east. The professor was from Puerto Rico and dark skies in August down there could mean hurricanes. I drove home in strange acid light, parked in the garage and shut its doors.

"Where is Fellow?" I called out to Dola from the back porch steps. "He doesn't come when I call and I know how he hates storms."

"You best find him," she said. "He getting old, been here most long as I been. He help me raise you. Go look every place."

Her voice blended with the first mumble of thunder and I turned away. My heart pounded as I ran to the front gates to see if they were closed. Wind whipped the oak trees until the leaves were horizontal, green hands beckoned me, pointing with shivery fingers. The roar of the storm became a vortex in my head. Thoughts whirled and circled, sounds pounded at my brain, grasped for a hold, then flew away again. Knocking, knocking--in the Greenery knocking. I ran toward it.

Fellow lay partially hidden in the vines with splashes of scarlet around him bold in the dim light. The knife that had slashed his throat angled in weeds as if dropped from above. I looked up and saw Claudia floating in mid-air, hovering like a wounded butterfly. The rope around her neck was tied to the largest branch of the tall oak. With each gust of wind her feet tapped against a plank Emory had nailed to the trunk long ago.

I knelt to stroke Fellow's head. "Forgive her," I said. "Please forgive her."

She had found our secret place. It would never be ours again.

Dola and Maybelle showed me the letter they found in Claudia's room before the police arrived with the ambulance.

My window looks directly into a mass of kudzu vines that smother and choke two large oak trees near the front fence. The vine draws life from the trees with its tendrils that squeeze juice out of the limbs and trunks as I have had blood squeezed out of me. The oaks wait where they were planted--as I have done. I sit here waiting in this goddam womb of a house. There is cruelty hidden in the walls, in keyholes where a blind eye stares and a deaf ear listens. The house comes alive with the night, then lies preening itself in sunlight like a cat. Like Miss Eugenie.

My mother's day began in the evening when my father walked in the front door. He looked at her with sheer love wiping away tired lines from his face. She killed him, of course. Her pampered selfishness killed him like a bullet through the brain. When her drunken brother lay passed out at the Dempsey Hotel for days with a prostitute, my father, sick himself with a cold, picked up that worthless Brandon reeking with blue blood and alcohol. Miss Eugenie hovered over them, Brandon draped over Daddy's shoulder like a limp shawl.

My beautiful Daddy's hacking cough led them all up the stairs.

Soon two doctors watched <u>him</u> around the clock. Two nurses, one at night and one in the day, looking out the window: "Who is that riding on horseback down Vineville Avenue? It's death I see coming and I cannot stop it. It rides slowly but it holds the reins steady while it approaches the gate."

Fellow moves around in the kudzu cave now as I write.

What does he expect to find in there, in the dim light that could have meant birth and new life but instead means green slime that grows on dead bones. He is looking for his Cady who left days ago, after she had lifted the curtain of leaves and led Willie Fosters inside. <u>My</u> Willie Fosters. I think he made love to her while I stood here and felt every touch. She was held and loved in pure green light. I cannot forgive her for that since I have lived in silence and darkness.

Fellow is moving around among the vines. The wind howls now and whips the trees. I see the flattened weeds where she held him. The sky lowers itself to hide the place but I know it is there.

It's time to leave my room and welcome the visitor who once again approaches the front gate and offer him shelter from the storm.

## Claudia

Dola and Maybelle sat with me on the back porch steps in air still heavy with clouds. My mother was in her upstairs sitting room with Reverend Randolph. "Ain't nobody never going to see this," Dola took the crumpled pages from me and stuffed them in her apron pocket. "This put all the blame on Miss Genie and it ain't fair."

"It wasn't my mother Claudia hated," the broad arms rocked me back and forth as they had in my childhood. "It was me."

Dola held my head to her shoulder. "Ain't nobody here to blame. You got to believe that, baby. Did I ever tell you a lie? Did I ever?"

"Dola, why did she have to hurt my Fellow?" I could not say the real word. Minutes later we heard Uncle Andrew's voice in the hall tell a policeman, "Miss Eugenie refuses to allow an autopsy and we must respect her wishes. The cause of death is obvious." As an after-thought he said, "Have someone dispose of the dog."

"No!" I jumped up and ran inside. "Don't you dare touch him. Not any one of you."

"Miss," the policeman said, "we'll see that the body is taken care of in the right way. Easy now. I've had dogs of my own."

"Don't you touch my Fellow!" I pushed his hand off my arm.

"Leave it be, sir," Dola spoke behind me. "Maybelle and me will take care of things in a little while."

"Yessir," Maybelle said. "Us'll take care of that."

The three of us sat again on the top step of the back porch. Dola held my head against the heady familiar smells of her chest --sour liquor fumes, snuff, pine straw, old newspapers, and hot sun on dusty red roads.

I leaned into the scent I had found comfort in since the first hour of my life.

"Oh, help me. Somebody please help me."

55

# CHAPTER 7

The piano at The Oaks was silent except when Maybelle dusted the keys. The house sat heavily on the land in end-of-summer stillness. Miss Eugenie's door remained closed.

"What can I do for her?" I asked Dola when she returned to the kitchen with another tray of untouched food. "She, of all people, knows we can't change the past."

"Her way ain't your way, baby."

"But it's just not healthy to lie up there like that."

"Lord God. You tell me one thing ever been healthy 'round this place and I give you a dollar."

I climbed the stairs and knocked on the door to my mother's room, then entered and sat at the foot of the bed. Her fingers rested on a brass crucifix Grandmother d'Autremont brought back to her from a trip to the south of France years ago. Her eye-lids fluttered and she moved the light blanket covering her, indicating I was welcome. September sun hovered in a pale sky. Organdy curtains moved at her windows and Joe Henry sang to himself as he crossed the back lawn to the old playhouse. It now held tools, a trunk full of discarded toys and two formidable hordes of memories, the old and the new, vying with each other for a winning position. Her hand reached out and touched mine.      "I wish you could have known your father longer," she said.

"I wish so, too."

"He would have wanted you to get away from Macon and The Oaks. I've been talking to the nuns at the Academy about a  college in Florida. You have to leave Georgia for awhile.

"Mother, I want to be near you."

"No, you must remove yourself from all this. I hear it's a good school. We'll begin getting you ready soon for the second semester."

"I can't imagine any life away from The Oaks. I was born in this room on this very bed."

"Of all my children, Cady, you are the most like me. It's a great help to know that. Somehow, wherever you are, you'll survive."

October tingled the senses with deep blue spicy afternoons. Leaves turned yellow and red and oppressive heat slunk away. I took long walks, fast-paced ones that filled my thoughts with the right placing of each footstep, mindless strides along Vineville Avenue, allowing myself to think only of autumn flower beds that matched the golden air.

One day I walked two miles to Redcliffs Cemetery. Claudia lay beneath a white marble slab with camellias carved around her name.

"These flowers should have been on her bridal gown, not her tombstone," my mother had said to me sometime after the funeral. I stared down at the grave and knew it had been reaching and waiting. Open-armed.

Sadness pounded at me as I sat between Daddy's stone and hers and watched wind take flowers from all the graves to scatter them at random, even down the hill to the Confederate tombstones by the Ocmulgee River which itself moved so slowly I wondered now if it were weary from seeing all this evidence of human folly.

Mother began to come downstairs for a few hours each day. She talked on the telephone to her favorite nun at the Academy several times a week and once took her for a drive through the autumn countryside.

She became almost animated when she received a letter from Emory at sea somewhere in the Pacific. He wrote that he wanted to go regular Navy as soon as possible and if they would have him.

"My wonderful, wonderful darling," Miss Eugenie held the letter against her chest. "He is like my people who founded this country, a lover of liberty to the marrow of his bones."

Emory enjoyed danger--taking chances on his horse, jumping fences and stone walls that almost involved flying even before he joined the Navy--and landing safely.

"Mother, he will be an admiral in ten years. I think it's the perfect career for him--made to order." A rare moment of terror in the air, long stretches sitting mindlessly on verandas of Officers' Clubs, drinking and seducing women, then flying sedately away when they hinted at anything serious. He was a true lover of liberty.

Life continued. Letters from Willie came five or six at a time. He was overseas, stationed somewhere in Iraq, and I kept his mail in a metal box in case The Oaks caught on fire. In a dry spell without hearing from him for days, I read each of them again beginning with the first letter all the way to the last.

In November, stronger winds began and northern gray skies settled in.

"Sherman's revenge," Miss Eugenie said.

"Revenge? He won, Mother. The Yankees won that war."

"No," she shook her head firmly. "They did not win. The South was never conquered, only overwhelmed."

"Is that how come us colored folks is still slaves so to speak?" Dola leaned her head in from the kitchen to the breakfast room where we were sitting with coffee.

"Dola," Miss Eugenie asked. "Would you like to help with the grocery list now?"

I watched Dola stuff the Thanksgiving turkey, "I do hope you have the integrity not to read my letters from Willie."

"Hoo! I don't know 'bout no integrity but if it's good, I got it. And I do hope you know I don't give no sweet damn 'bout them letters. Only thing worries me is you not being in school. Eula Belle's in Atlanta studying hard all the time, you just moping 'round this house full of ghosts."

"I'm taking a semester off to be with Mother. I'll go back soon, I promise."

One afternoon I noticed orange and yellow chrysanthemums on the dining room table as I walked into the kitchen to tell Dola I was home from my long walk.

"The house looks beautiful," I said.

"We got company coming."

"Company? Here? Miss Eugenie is having a dinner guest?"

"She is."

"Well, who? It must be the angel Gabriel."

"Close, but that ain't it. It's one of them black men, you know, one of them mumbo-jumbo men all the time wears black from your old school."

"Do you mean a Catholic priest is coming to dinner?"

"Yeah. That's what I done told you already."

Father Delereaux, a dark-haired handsome man who told us he grew up in New Orleans, showed he was well-versed in the riposte demanded by Southern Belleism. His smiling witticisms provided the foil for Miss Eugenie's coyness and delicate posturing throughout the four-course meal.

We had coffee and brandy in my father's study after dinner. A small and intimate room, it immediately became a cyclone that battered me in a whirlwind of emotions. Until this night it was a closed door I walked by quickly, sometimes stopping to put my hand against the grain of the wood, once opening it to the faded odor of pipe tobacco that caused me to run to another room and collapse on a chair with images scattering by me like fallen linden leaves.

"Cady, please. Father Delereaux is speaking to you."

I turned my face toward him.

"We'll make it a hasty course of instructions but they'll give you all the essentials," he was saying.

"Essentials?"

"You and I are going to become Catholics." Serenity masked Miss Eugenie's face but her eyes glowed. "We are moving through the narrow door that separates Episcopalians from Roman Catholics into a joyous haven. I'm certain we'll find a balm there for the blows life has dealt us. Now tell me, Father, when shall we begin?"

When I went upstairs I took the book he left with me to read in bed.

BALTIMORE CATECHISM

PAGE ONE:

Question: Who made the world?

Answer: God made the world.

Question: Who is God?

Answer: God is the creator of Heaven and Earth and of all things.

Question: Why did God make me?

Answer: God made me to love Him and serve Him in this world and to be happy with Him in the next.


The next? The book slipped to the floor as I turned off the light. I stared at the flickering ceiling alive with oak shadows. Willie, Willie, hurry home. You are the only haven I want anywhere, anytime.

Before I fell asleep I remembered my mother's face. In the light from the desk lamp that had lit the small den with an amber halo, she looked almost happy in this world.

# CHAPTER 8

The day after New Year's I shivered on my walk along a bleak Vineville Avenue with smoke from chimneys of the old homes blending into a stone gray sky. I entered our front door to a house frozen in silence like a time-worn portrait dim with faded colors. My mother sat in the living room by the fireplace with a tea tray in front of her while Dola and Maybelle bent to serve two awkward strangers who sat across the room on the smaller couch. The woman held her hands stiffly folded in her lap; on closer look her small brown straw hat quivered. The portrait jumped to life when the man turned to look at me out of startling blue eyes, familiar enough to make my heart pound. He rose, his new suit stiffly apart from his tall lanky frame.

"Mr. and Mrs. Fosters, this is my daughter, Cady, a long-time friend of Willie's," Miss Eugenie said.

I shook hands with each of them, trembling. "Have you news of Willie?"

"Yes, they have, Cady, and you can help me reassure them that everything will be all right. The War Department sent a telegram that Willie is missing in action. His plane is probably overdue but as we all know, that could mean he's unable to get in touch with his Base at the moment."

After the words "missing in action" my breathing changed. I sat beside my mother on the sofa unable to hold a cup of tea but nodded "yes, of course" and "by all means" to her chatter that whirled around my ears like hornets. Finally Maybelle walked the visitors to the front door. Mother followed them to their truck.

"We'll all hear soon. Please call me at any time." After they drove away she went upstairs to her room without looking back and closed the door.

Dola stood in the passage between the hall and the dining room. I walked into her open arms and put my head on her shoulder.

"Why?" I asked her.

"Why? Now there's a word you got to forget. I ask it myself first time I seen my skin was darker than the white folks." She put one palm against the middle of my back and moved me into the kitchen.

"Come set over here and let's have us a little special tea." It fell into my stomach like a burning coal, warming my whole body. Frozen tears inside me melted on my face.

"This color skin rule my whole life but it wont the color that fixed me in this rut--it be the minds of the other folks. All this meanness--this killing. It don't make no sense."

"Will it ever stop?"

"Naw," she added more rum to each tea cup. "It ain't never go' stop. But you gets used to it. Almost."

My whole body shivered that night on the back porch steps with Dola and Joe Henry.

"I'm saying he ain't dead. I'm saying he down on the ground somewhere hiding in some bushes like in the desert or a dirt-made house," Joe Henry said.

"That's right," Dola poked my ribs with her elbow. "You listen to Joe Henry now. He one smart man. Ain't I always said Joe Henry smart? He tell you the truth ever' time, so you listen.

"I'm listening. Oh, dear Heaven, I'm listening hard."

In the middle of January Dola and Maybelle rode with me in a taxi to Union Station at the far end of Cherry Street.

"I don't want to go to Florida," I told them. Dola held one of my hands in both of hers and patted it all the way to downtown Macon.

"You gots to get away from this town 'til the stink of death done gone from you. Bake yourself in the sun. And remember . . . there's a reason why your two eyes is set in front of your head. That's so you can't look backwards."

Tears too close to the surface kept me from telling my most cherished belongings how I felt about them--they did belong to me in the realest sense of the word.

When the train began to move I looked over my right shoulder at tracks leading back to the graves on the hill by the Ocmulgee River beyond my sight. So long, fellows, I waved toward the Confederate graves. Lots of people have a dream that dies. Even General Sherman made sense once when he said "War is hell".

# CHAPTER 9

Three men in uniform tried to pick me up when I changed trains in Jacksonville. The handsome Navy officer, with blond hair and perfect teeth, actually made me laugh mocking my Southern accent as we waited together for the Miami connection. Eric Sorensen wore the two and a half-stripes of a Lieutenant Commander on his epaulets. He looked less than twenty-five. I told him I was going to school near Miami to finish my junior year in college.

"I hope they have good food," he said "You're a little on the thin side."

"I've had a bad cold I couldn't shake. That's why I'm going south for the rest of the winter."

He called before I unpacked.


"It's beautiful here--lots of green lawns and Spanish-type buildings, a great swimming pool and two tennis courts," I said. "But it's strict. I can't leave the campus with a date until the Dean meets him and approves."

"No problem there," he said. "All women love me."

"Oh?"

"Well, they have to know me a little first."

Mary Theresa Muscato from Grosse Point Park, Michigan, had the room next to mine in the upperclass-women's dormitory. I watched her unpack her two trunks in contrast to my three suitcases. When she came to the end of the cashmere sweaters and cruise clothes and reached into the bottom layer of the last trunk, she lifted two lengths of spidery black lace and laid them reverently in her top dresser drawer.

"Pretty. What are they?" I asked.

"They're mantillas to put over my head at daily Mass so I don't have to bother with a hat or beret so early in the morning. This one belonged to my grandmother."

"Daily Mass?"

"Yes. You may borrow one since you don't have any."

"What time is daily Mass?"

"Six-thirty--before breakfast, of course. That's the way it's always done in Catholic boarding schools. A nun comes to each room ringing a little hand bell about five-thirty."

I remembered Joe Henry bending over our fireplaces at dawn to warm our room before we got up. "You mean you get up at five-thirty every day?"

She stared at me. "Don't you want to receive as often as possible?"

"Receive what?"

"Holy Communion--the Body and Blood of our Lord Jesus Christ, God Himself. What kind of instructions to join the Church did you get?"

"Not many. And to tell the truth, they were really for my mother. I didn't listen very well because I had something big on my mind." I wondered why I had to get up out of bed to receive God. "What if I just talk to Him quietly by myself?"

Mary Theresa shook her head. "What kind of place is May-con, Georgia? You must come from the sticks! You'll never make Red Birds if you talk like that."

"What is Red Birds?" The reference to May-con, Georgia, was unimportant; Grosse Point Park in Michigan was foreign country to me.

"I got it through the grapevine. Sotto voce. It's a secret sorority--very hush-hush. The nuns aren't supposed to know but Anna Marie probably heard about it and told them."

"Which one is Anna Marie?"

"She sat across from you in the dining hall at lunch. You can't miss her--European, long blonde hair, gorgeous clothes. A goody-goody and a snitch."

"With a heavy accent?"

"That's funny coming from you, Corn Pone. Yah, she haf zee havvy accent from Svitzerlund. She and her mother are riding out the war in New York. She wants to be a nun."

"Tell me more about the Red Birds."

"The club's named after the Cardinals who really run the Church--you can figure that one out. From what I can tell the requirements are Catholic, money, good looks, good clothes."

"I'm a little short on some of those," I said. "How about `family'?"

"Family? What do you mean?"

"Never mind. Anyway, I've only been a Catholic for three weeks. My mother made me join."

"Didn't you want to? It's a very special gift."

"Well--I felt okay as an Episcopalian. It was right for me." Saint Matthew's was filled with a delicate scent I had relished each time I opened its doors. Hymnals carried it as if they had been held by perfumed ladies of the first Elizabeth's court. Pews were havens of familiarity with an aura of history and a gentle God. "I'm sorry. I can't help it--I'm really not a Catholic."

Marie Theresa shrugged. "We've lasted for centuries without the Southern hicks invading our ranks."

I excused myself and went back to my room. Miss Eugenie was right when she said I was like her.

"What did you say your last name was?" One of the seniors, a girl with black hair named Maurine O'Connor asked me at dinner.

"Worthington."

"British, isn't it?" She looked at the others seated around her.

"A long time ago some of my ancestors came to this country from England."

"Well, don't worry your little head. Nobody's perfect."

# CHAPTER 10

Commander Eric Sorensen waited for me on Saturday afternnon in the lobby of the Miami Inter Continental Hotel. He leapt up from one of the plush velveteen couches, his tan stark against the white flash of greeting in his Navy dress uniform. Eric's smile stayed in his gold-colored eyes and I uncoiled as we sat in the Shell Room for Tom Collinses. His conversation was a marvel of gliding over surfaces, swooping and heading away from anything serious or remotely heavy. It led me away from my sadness.

"I'm glad I came today," I said. "I almost didn't, you know." His face was startled, blank. "I'm expecting a long distance call from my mother about an old friend. And lots of other reasons, really. Georgia is--well, a different world. I think about it a lot." I had never been in a restaurant with Willie, never looked across a table at him.

"Hey, none of that. No homesickness here." He signalled the waiter. "Two more," he said. "Happy times ahead - for both of us."

At dinner I learned his family lived in San Francisco. His only sister was a west-coast "socialite" married to a surgeon. The word socialite was new to me and somehow I felt Miss Eugenie would not approve.

My vocabulary grew at St. Catherine. Sitting by the swimming pool with friends the first Friday afternoon after classes I watched a group of nuns walk past us in their distinctive movement like ice skaters sliding by in flat unison.

I turned to Mary Theresa covering herself with baby oil and iodine for a deeper suntan. "Sister Loretta is cute," I said. "She must be less than twenty-five and I'll bet she's really good looking under that veil and all those robes."

"Miss McGill thinks so, too."

"Miss McGill, the tennis instructor? What do you mean?"

"Oh, Cady, you <u>are</u> dumb. Haven't you noticed? The rest of us have."

"Noticed what?"

"They're usually together. We think the two of them are -- you know. Girls who like girls instead of boys." Mary Theresa said.

I thought awhile. I had heard a word somewhere but I couldn't remember what it was. "Surely--not a nun?"

"Okay, Miss McGill, then."

"You're impossible to believe, Cady," Cissy Petusak spoke from the edge of the pool where she lay on a huge towel. "Georgia must be without a doubt the bung-hole of the forty-eight states."

Later, after lights-out, I stared up at the dark. What was that word that meant girls liking girls and what was a bung-hole?

"Okay, so you're dumb with absolutely not one ounce of sophistication but--you're damn good-looking and how could we do without that cornfed accent. Daisy Mae, 'we all' welcome you to Red Birds," Maureen O'Connor said to me two weeks later on the bus taking the upperclassmen to downtown Miami.

"Whee," I said. For an instant I saw Claudia leaning against a telephone pole on Vineville Avenue with her eyes closed to a bright beautiful world she would not be part of. Could it have been less than two years ago?

Wheezy Callahan from Boston burned a foul-smelling powder in her bathroom every mid-night when her asthma attacks began. It made a cover-up for smoking our forbidden cigarettes after we piled seven or eight deep into the small room, sitting in the shower, on the back of the toilet and huddled on the floor in our pajamas. We talked in whispers while Wheezy coughed under the towel she threw over her head to breathe the dried mixture from a bowl beneath her face.

"What is that?" I asked the first time.

"It's a special herb that grows only in New England in the Green Mountains and it helps. My mother mails me one or two cans a month," she said between gasps.

"Special herb, my ass," Cissy said. "It's horse manure, pure and simple. Horrible." Cissy was a large athletic girl whose father bred race horses near Alliance, Ohio. "My family can keep you supplied with that for the rest of your life." She took several deep drags on her cigarette. We all looked like disembodied faces floating in a fallen cloud.

Maureen O'Connor settled herself in Wheezy's bathroom with two bath towels folded behind her back. "Imagine being a virgin all of your life like these nuns," she said. "Did I tell you Pelham Stewart and I are being married in late June in South Hampton?"

"Only fifty times at last count," Mary Theresa handed out bottles of beer she had brought into the dormitory late in the afternoon hidden in a large Kotex box and kept cool in her bathtub. "He's fantastic, terribly handsome and I've loved him since I was a child," Maureen said. "I used to watch him sail by on the Sound. I can't believe we are really going to do it on our wedding night--it'll be so great to have it happen for the first time with someone you've loved since you were just a little kid."

I threw my head back to take another swallow of beer. "I think I choked," I said, wiping away tears running down my face.

In the middle of March, Eric left for four-week temporary-duty in Natal, Brazil. I missed the cheerful stories about his childhood. He told me he had his own sailboat, a sloop, by the time he was ten and the waters around northern California bordered his world. "It was my living space," he said.

"Your parents sound great," I said. "You had a lot of freedom my sister and I didn't have".

"Lord, yes--my sister and I only saw our parents at dinner and by then they were always pretty cheerful--downright funny, you might say, after two double martinis." His light-hearted company cushioned the deep ache of thinking about the sadness in Georgia that slammed against me at intervals. Unbending routine at St. Catherine became a protective shield until an unexpected pause shattered me like the thinnest of crystals.

Miami was a different world from Macon. Its excitement and pace touched me after a few weekends.

All of the boarders at St. Catherine's were allowed to go into town at noon on Saturday, the upperclassmen without a chaperone. After lunch and a movie we went to a good restaurant in Coconut Grove on the pretext of having dinner. Three or four steps into Monty's open-air restaurant and bar, young men of every nationality surrounded us. Gradually, the chrysalis covering me peeled back a little. Life, even felt with shaking fingers, was precious and Miami in 2002 was its core. Today, it shouted. This hour, this minute. Taste it. Feel the rhythm of the great collective pulse. Live, live. Tomorrow we may --but I never let myself finish the thought. Youth, in this yellow land of rattling palms and blue water, would never end. Later, standing on the corner of Biscayne Boulevard and Flagler Street looking west was like being at the bend of a jaunty river of people wearing every color of the rainbow, weaving and bobbing in a solid stream toward Biscayne Bay. I watched them with my friends from St. Catherine's, all Yankee girls with two living parents and no suicides in their backgrounds. Awareness of the fragility of being alive in that place at that moment flooded me. In the urgency of hundreds of young faces coming toward us in constant motion, time itself halted. There might not be a tomorrow--could it not be there had never been a yesterday? The rest of the world to the north and across the ocean were unrealities, and I was a piece of flamingo-pink confetti dancing dizzily under a lemon-colored sky.

# CHAPTER 11

Four months. Nobody is missing for four months. Willie would have crawled, crept, clawed for help someway. Amnesia? No, he had dog tags and finger prints. A prisoner of war perhaps? His Air Wing Helicopter Squadron commander would know somehow. He was dead, splattered against the sky by a direct hit of enemy fire, unrecognizable bones drifting to the ground with a melted metal necklace spiraling leisurely beside him.

Was Claudia having the final seductive laugh, embracing him in death beyond my reach? Be good to him, I asked her. Smooth his ruffled brown hair. Gentle him with your stiff dead fingers.

Mary Theresa and Patty Collins came running from their rooms; Sister Loretta stood in the open door. "You are disturbing the entire floor," she said.

Nuns had their heads covered even in the middle of the night I noticed.

"I'm sorry," I said. "I had a terrible nightmare."

"I'll sit here awhile," Mary Theresa said. "It's Willie, isn't it?" she asked when we were alone.

I nodded face down into my pillow. "Thank you for staying."


My dear Cady:

I hear from Mother Marietta regularly that you are doing well in your studies and adjusting to dormitory life in good fashion. I am not surprised as I always expect excellence from you in every endeavor. It is bred into you to conduct yourself in an exemplary manner; therefore, I am writing this letter in the belief that you will react to life's unexpected as your inherent instincts dictate.

Willie Foster's father stopped by this morning. He has received a letter from Colonel Johnathan Lamb to the effect that the huge helicopter in which his son was being transferred, was last seen near but not over Bagdad and did not return to Base. All members on that flight are now officially classified "missing and presumed dead." I know that you and he have been friends since your early years and whatever the outcome we will remember his gentleness and kindness to each of us. The address of Mr. and Mrs. James Leroy Fosters is 10 General Meade Street, McMartin Textile Company. I am sure they would appreciate an encouraging note from you.

We are well, although the silence in the house is overwhelming. How quickly things change but our lives are but a blink of an eye in God's time. I commend you to Him.

With love,

Mother

P.S. Dola said to tell you her skin is wearing black for you. It seems a tasteless remark but I promised her I'd include it in this letter.

A perky freshman stood at my door, excitement radiating from her scrubbed face. "Sister Josephine wants to know why you aren't at Mass? She's really mad that you're not in Chapel--this is Sunday, you know!"

Because there is no God.

"Cady, did you hear me?"

Tell that fat penguin I've lost my flesh-and-blood love. She won't know what man-love is but tell her that for a brief pause of time I walked with the angels under kudzu vines. I don't want to go to any other heaven.

"Cady?"

"Tell Sister Josephine I'm not feeling well and I will not be in Chapel today."


I pushed aside the curtains later that night and looked out over the swimming pool that cast its dimmed other-worldly glow over empty lawn furniture. Surrounding grass was awake. Gardenia and jasmine scrubs breathed heavily into the night air. They carried new life in their veins, flaunting their fecundity. Willie, Willie, whatever happened, I hope there was no suffering. I cannot imagine that you were afraid but how you must have hated knowing that death was coming to rob you and me of belonging.

I was compassed for a month for missing Sunday Mass--no weekend privileges, no walk to the Causeway for a hamburger and a Coca Cola after class on week days. No Vineville Avenue to stride along encompassed in a warm womb of the familiar.

Red Birds gathered around me. "Cady, how can we help you?"

"Look, this will pass."

"Boys are dying all over the world and most of them had a girl waiting somewhere like you."

"I lit a candle and offered my Mass for Willie."

"I'm saying a rosary every day for you."

"Sister Jo is a jerk to pen you in like this. Can't we tell her what happened?"

"No, please." Would it make any difference? "You've all been so kind but I really just want to be alone."

Three weeks later on a Saturday afternoon I was called down to the weekend silence of the first floor. I noticed a flush on the face of the young nun who had day-duty in the dormitory as she sat at the desk at the foot of the stairs. "There's a delightful young man waiting for you in the drawing room."

Eric Sorensen stood in the curve of wide bay windows silhouetted in Florida spring abundance outside. Tall, handsome, golden.

I extended my hand to welcome him but felt my face pulled to his chest, crushed in smells of clean sunbaked skin, the scent of soap and after shave lotion.

We walked past the swimming pool, under blue Moorish arches of the dining hall, up tiled steps to the Torch Porch, the one place on campus where smoking was allowed. We sat on the long veranda overlooking a sea of purple-tipped grass that swept out to a fringe of Florida pines.

"I'm off to a new duty station in a month," he said. My family sent me a fat check for a farewell-to-Miami present."

"Great, Eric. Take it and have fun with a girl who isn't always in the doldrums."

"I'll bet I can talk the nuns into letting up on you. We could go somewhere for dinner."

The afternoon floated in a light blue haze of late March, blooming bougainvillea, and hibiscus, with palm fronds clapping hands of encouragement, snapping their dried skirts to awake me to life.

"Try, if you like," I said. "I would love to help you celebrate." He was handsome, this golden boy. And alive.

We went to a small restaurant near the 79th Street Causeway bridge. Tables glowed with pink lampshades and daiquiris intensified the exotic accents of tropical music from a small band with a fantastic guitarist. "Brazil, where hearts are entertaining June, we stood beneath an amber moon and softly whispered 'someday soon'"—a good old love song.

We danced well together.

After dinner we stood on the bridge and looked at the city south of us, each building defiant against the sky. Stars were bright enough to have led a dozen German submarines to our shores during WWII.

"I can't leave you, Cady, without knowing I mean something to you. You're different from any girl I've ever known. I think I'm in love with you."

"Don't be in love, Eric. I've heard it's deadly."

He was due to leave the last week in April for duty in Jacksonville. Mother Marietta lifted my remaining restriction and I refused all invitations for dates but his. During that late spring month we moved in the rarefied atmosphere of racing time. Each detail of what I heard him say, what I tasted and touched, stood out with incredible clarity. We kissed well together. And often.

End-of-the-term good-byes to the Red Birds were easier because of their excitement in getting back to their preppy beaux and a summer of party-fun waiting for them in their gleaming Yankee homes.

"Write lots."

"Tell all the news."

"Don't hold back anything even if you blush to see it on paper."

"Try to be good."

"To hell with that."

"Cissy, don't forget. You ride the horses, not vice versa."

"Mary Theresa, please lay off the pasta. Your boobs are big enough."

"Keep those chastity belts locked, girls, I mean that."

"Speak for yourself, toots."

"God bless you!"

# CHAPTER 12

The United States Navy "planned" our wedding. Eric's arrival in Macon for our small ceremony depended on the weather in Florida and how many flight hours he completed before he was granted leave. Miss Eugenie and I had twenty-four hours after his phone call to prepare the chapel in the priest's house at Immaculate Conception Parish. I didn't know exactly what "Immaculate Conception" meant but I hoped it wasn't a bad omen.

Eric was Protestant; we could not be married in the body of any Catholic Church and the Bishop of the Catholic See in Georgia forbade all home weddings. My girlhood dream of walking down the stairs on the arm of one of my two uncles to stand before a flowerbanked fireplace in the living room, witnessed by six oaks hiding their emotions in regal dignity, lay quenched as black ashes. Eric and I entered a small room in the priest's rectory together and heard Latin phrases bind us in an everlasting Sacrament. We said our vows in English before a dozen old girlhood friends of Miss Eugenie's. Back at The Oaks, Miss Pridey Buckingham, who came out of her cocoon for our wedding, held me close to her for a minute. "I've been a spinster all my life, Cady. You know I lost my only love in the last war--now you be happy for me, you hear?"

"I will, Miss Pridey. I really will!"

Dola and Maybelle served wine from the cellar. Before we said our goodbyes, Dola pulled me into the kitchen.

"I 'spect to hear from you a heap. And don't tell me no lies. Ever since you was born I always knowed when you was speaking true."

"What would I have to fib about?"

"Nothing, I hope. Just remember I changed your didies. That's all I got to say 'cept I want you to be happy."

I hugged her. "I already am."

She pulled me over to the window and held my face in the light. "That's better," she said.

"What's better?"

"The sadness done gone some from your eyes."

Miss Eugenie gave us a second-hand Ford Taurus for our wedding gift. We drove to Atlanta before dark our first night together.

So life was an exchange. Tenderness, wordlessness that I once heard in my deepest places were traded for wild machinations, soaring outpourings of sensuality. I was free to call out words I didn't know I knew. On the other side of a brave new door, I promised myself to shut it and keep it locked.

The old red brick in Norfolk was slippery with rain but it caught and held one last ray of the sun. The hotel had crouched on that corner in Virginia through two wars before this one. During the first, cannons rumbled past it, pulled by dying men carrying a dying flag. I wanted to tell Eric about that tragic time but I didn't think he would understand.

His eyes looked green above his green Naval Aviator's uniform, green like a shallow pool that was filled with tree shadows. If he had been wearing khakis, his eyes would be beige like barren sand. I did not know then what was beneath the color-changes in his eyes. We knew only the surfaces of each other.

I did not have to turn around from the window in our room to know that he was standing a few feet behind me. I saw him through my shoulder blades, through the length of my spine that was straight and knobby and prickling with pinpoints as I watched the old red bricks fade and I knew he was about to reach for me. I knew this but I stayed at the window. Through the angles of the buildings in the next few blocks, I saw a sliver of the Bay, dark gray and pockmarked with rain. I saw the prow of a battleship with white numbers painted on the side, steady in the water, heavy with power and cunning. Behind it, others lined up like vicious trained dogs eager to kill, squat and ugly, waiting for the signal to attack. "Go ahead, try me," they were saying to the waves that reached to touch them and slithered back timidly. He had been my bridegroom for five days. In time he would become a husband, maybe a father someday. But not then. At that moment I needed him to be the other half of me.

The only light in the room was from the whiteness of the bed sheet we were lying on--the top one was kicked off and lay on the floor with the blankets. We touched sides from ankle-bones to shoulders, every inch pressing against the other. Eric reached for a cigarette somewhere in the dark with his left hand, the last one in the pack, he told me. When I inhaled, I felt a cold in my throat and knew it was a Salem; my favorite. The red glow at the end arched between us as he took a drag and handed it to me.

"Hopefully we'll be able to find a nice apartment somewhere in Norfolk close to the Base." he said.

Dear God in Heaven, I had never even turned on a stove. We knew so little about each other. After a few minutes I was brave enough to say those words out loud.

"You have about two months to learn," I heard him smiling up at the ceiling.

It turned out to be three. The late Virginia autumn made a quarter circle into a winter of my first snow fall.

We had found a one bedroom apartment with a nice, but small kitchen where I would have to cook my first meal.

One December afternoon at 1:30, he held me close to him on a taxi-strip beside a gray jet with a blue star on its side. I saw behind the green pools in his eyes and I read the words he could not say above the noise of the engines of planes taxing nearby. He backed away suddenly and climbed  the ladder into the cockpit. He was gone. The "me" he left behind stood on the ground patched with ice puddles and watched until the gray plane flew into a far-away cloud and disappeared toward another airbase, a carrier, or some other country.

# CHAPTER 13

Miss Eugenie spoke on the telephone in her firmest voice. "I'm leaving at once for Norfolk. A young girl cannot possibly drive that long distance alone."

"Mother, I'm not exactly a 'young girl' anymore." My voice shook a little. "I'm Mrs. Eric Sorensen. Besides, some of the other Navy wives and I have talked about finding a place to rent, maybe on Virginia Beach. All of us will be waiting the return of the squadron. Each of the pilots are in Eric's squadron and we could help each other get through loneliness without them."

"Simply out of the question. I'll wire you what time to meet my train. Stay in your room until I get there." She ended the connection by hanging up.

I explained to the others why I couldn't be a part of their plan. "My mother wants me to come home. It won't be easy being with her again."

The trees on the low hills were bare when we drove into Macon from Atlanta in a rented car. We passed Uncle Stephen's house behind two acres of lawn rising to its creamy stuccoed splendor in the Rivoli section. "He seems to be enjoying our money quite well; money that should have been yours, Mother, after Daddy died," I said. Miss Eugenie froze into silence. Money--anyone's money--was high on her list of forbidden topics, followed by any mention of sex. I wondered about Eric's mother. Her pleasant letters made me want to meet her. She sounded modern in her attitudes and sophisticated. The ambiance of The Oaks was the past. San Francisco, with its energetic, ambitious populace would be more in touch with the reality of 2004.

Dola met us at the front door and held me, patting my back for a long time. "Hoo! I's real glad you come home. Even the ghosts done left this place it been so boring."

When Miss Eugenie went upstairs for her prayer-time on the prie-dieu in her sitting room, I sank into a chair at the kitchen table as if I were falling into the arms of a lost friend.

"What's that you got in your hand?" Dola asked when she brought two cups of special tea and put them down beside us.

"It's called a cigarette."

"I know damn well what it's name be but how come you's holding one?"

I slowly lit my cigarette and inhaled. "That's why."

She grabbed the rest of the package. "Gimme them things. Your mama ain't going to like that from you."

I sipped my tea. "You're not making any sense, Dola. You've always acted like you thought my mother was a little bit crazy."

"That's the truth. Her kind ain't easy to be around but it just so happens I want you to be a lady and that means watching and listening to your mama. You got a whole lot riding on your shoulders."

I took a long drag and exhaled slowly. "What, pray tell?"

"This family--and what it going to be in the next hundred years. You is Miss Eugenie living on. It was always too late for Ermory and Claudia. They never had no chance after Mr. Sam died."

"And I did?" Willie was presumed dead, Eric was somewhere I didn't know about, and The Oaks looked shabbier than ever. The quicksand of my mother's authority had pulled at me during our train trip and drive from Atlanta, silent and relentless, erasing my new adult identity.

"If it would bother Miss Eugenie, I'll stop. Take the damn cigarettes. I only smoked because everyone else did in the Navy."

"Well, we ain't got no Navy here. The Ocmulgee River ain't deep enough for nothing but catfish."

The first week home I followed a stray cat, probably from the cotton mill around the old play house. I sat on the back porch steps and held her.

Her purring told me she welcomed love wherever she found it. I looked around at the oak trees settling into winter and stroked her. "You and me, babe," I said.

# CHAPTER 14

Dola and I heard mother's high-pitched squeal from where we sat on the back porch watching December sun send full shafts of colors through the bare chinaberry tree. We turned to each other.

"Some person of the male sex is standing on our front porch," I said.

"You is speaking true. I's praying it ain't who I think it is,"

In a minute Emory stood on the back porch, tanned and trim in his Navy khakis. He bowed low to us with the visored hat of a full lieutenant sweeping in a wide arc before him.

"Isn't this the most fantastic surprise?" Miss Eugenie found her way to a back-porch chair and fell into it, her hands clasped against her chest. "What a gracious, good and kindly God we have to bring my precious son home safely to me."

I whispered to him as I kissed him on the cheek. "How safe are you, Emory? Have you been tested for a social disease lately?"

"So you've jumped over the broom," he said. "Was it good?"

"Now you all come on inside out of the cold and we'll have a teeny, tiny toast for this blessed, blessed day. Dola, don't you wish we had a fatted calf?"

"I wisht we had even a skinny one. Emory, my boy, you surely done brung your big fat wallet home, sir, I hope. And what other goodies have you brung with you for Miss Eugenie and Mrs. Sorenson?"

"Myself, of course!" he said. "Don't you all worry your heads about anything. A man is in the house now for a little while."

"Oh?" I whispered to Dola following them down the hall. "Where is he?"

"Show him to me, too," she yelled.

A week later she told me she wished she could leave Macon to visit her niece Eula Belle in Hapeville for a few days.

"Go ahead," I said. "If I can fix meals on a lousy stove in Norfolk, Virginia, not always well-received, mind you, I can take care of Mother and Emory in this big old kitchen."

Dola led me to the front driveway. Miss Eugenie's car was parked on the lawn, the right front wheel crushing her bare rose beds. "See? I can't go nowhere."

"Why did Emory park on the grass like this?"

"'Cause the grass was there."

"But we have a perfectly good garage."

"Nothing to do with what we got. Ain't no rules can hold Mr. Emory. He carrying on now with all kinds of women, I done hear. All kinds, all colors."

"Dola, we don't have but two colors in Macon--black and white."

"That ain't so. We got some sparky high yellows."

"You mean Emory is going out with mulatto girls?"

"Going out with a real bad one and sneaking her up the back stairs."

I stared at her. "Does Miss Eugenie know?"

Dola pushed her foot against grass flattened by the tires. "Hard to tell how much your mama knows. 'Thinking' don't leave no trail."

"I'll speak to him. I don't care what he does anywhere else but he can't use The Oaks for his sneaky purposes. It's not fair. Daddy's dead and sometimes I think Miss Eugenie died with him."

"Sometimes? Hoo!"

"Well, I'm still alive!"


When I saw Emory turn Mother's car into the driveway I waved him to a stop and climbed in the front seat. He looked to be in Stage One of his drinking--probably two bourbons and water.

"I know about your house guest", I said, "and your slumber parties."

He laughed. "That's one advantage to dark skin. You can hide in shadows. Tell busy-body Dola to mind her own damn business. This is my house, not hers.

"No, it isn't anybody's. This house belongs to our history and you damn well better remember that. Right or wrong, The Oaks is our past and you're not going to degrade us with your tacky shenanigans."

"Um-m-m. Not as tacky as you might think. In fact, pretty classy, I'd say."

"How dare you bring a prostitute home? And with Miss Eugenie's room down the hall."

"Mind your own business, Cady. And tell that black bitch if she wants to keep her job she'll keep quiet."

"You bastard. Here are my terms and you'd better listen. I'll be on watch and if you bring another street woman--black, green or purple--into this house I'll tell Uncle Andrew. And you know he's of the old school. He'll write to your commanding officer about your morals. Then you can just sit back on your worthless ass and wait twenty years for another promotion."

We stared at each other. He reached beyond my shoulder, opened the car door on my side and pushed me out with both hands. I hung onto the handle to keep from falling, then lowered myself to the grass. "You son of a bitch. Just try it once more."

"I'm glad you done that," Dola said when I told her about it. "Be good to your mama. Put up with her ways. Truth is, she ain't so well these days. She going to see Dr. Parker some. It's the lady-trouble."

In my twenty-one years I had never thought of Miss Eugenie as a physical being with everyday functions like the rest of the world. When I was thirteen I had found a book by my bed written by the Kotex company titled "Margorie May's Twelfth Birthday" with a simple explanation of the menstrual cycle. When I asked Claudia about it she laughed and called it "The Menace".

"When will it happen to me?" I asked. " When will it come?"

"It's when it doesn't come that life is hellish."

"What do you mean?"

She had laughed again while she lit a cigarette with wobbly fingers.

Until this moment Miss Eugenie's sense of privacy separated her in my mind from flesh-and-blood people. Shock and fright startled me.

"Is Miss Eugenie really sick?"

"No telling. She don't talk. I don't ask." Dola shook her head. "But you ain't looking too good yourself. How come you ain't told nobody there's a baby inside you. Not even me."

I squeezed her arm. "I was going to tell you when we were sitting on the back porch together the day Emory arrived. I quess I didn't want to share it while he was here."

"Don't you worry yo'self 'bout nothing, you hear me? I take care of things now."

Emory left in a taxi two days later with prayerful but restrained good-byes from Miss Eugenie.

She slowly climbed the stairs to her room. "My poor darling," she said. "His father died so young and I'm afraid I've been a poor substitute."

"Bullshit," Dola said when her door closed. "Not even Jesus riding in on a cloud wouldn't have made no difference in that boy. He's plain rotten."

# CHAPTER 15

I made an appointment with Dr. Parker the next day.

"Try to rest your mind about everything now, Miss Cady. Your husband will probably be home in time for the birth."

"I had sort of a fall yesterday."

"You're fine. Coming right along."

"My mother--how is she?"

"Miss Eugenie's going to spoil this child something awful, I bet."

"Especially if it's a dark-haired boy?"

Dr. Parker missed on his prediction. Samuel Beauregard Sorensen was a month old before his father came home. By then his name had evolved to "Sambeau".

"That ain't no name for no white child with yellow fuzz on his head and blue eyes. It don't fit," Dola said.

"Well, Dola, it fell over him like a mosquito net and `Sambeau' it is."


A long distance call from New York awoke me in the middle of the night the second week in June. "I'm catching the first hop to Atlanta, darling, then I'll come by train to Macon. I'll call you from the station."

"Wait until you see your son," I said.

Two days later Miss Eugenie and Dola blended into the faded background of The Oaks when we arrived home from the station in late afternoon. "Good Lord, he's handsome," Eric repeated over and over. "My parents are going to go ape over this baby. He's the image of Dad's people."

"A tall blonde Swede named Sambeau. Seems right, don't you think?" I asked.

"I think you're looking pretty much 'right' yourself," Eric said.

Miss Eugenie and Dola took the baby while Eric and I sat in the living room with tall drinks of Vodka and tonic.

He looked out at the trees in full leaf. "Same old place. You Southerners are really something!" he said. "Stubborn as hell. Anyone else would have moved to a smaller place and sold all this. The land itself must be priceless."

A cold dripping silver ice bucket provided us with an unknown number of drinks. Our fingers reached, and clung. Later I felt as if I were being wrapped slowly in velvet. Rich touches woke parts of me that had been numb for months. Candles on the table were flickering when I fell asleep with my face pressed against Eric's chest. The deep tan color had faded from his skin but I drifted in a sun-baked sheltered haven.

# CHAPTER 16

We left for San Francisco the next week to see Eric's family. Sambeau rode in a laundry basket on the back seat. Driving from Georgia to California became tedious as scenery changed to unadorned lands of the Middle West.

"My parents' roots are in this country," Eric said. "The Plains States."

"They're plain, all right." He turned from the driver's seat to stare at me. "What I meant was it's plain to see why you love them."

"Wait until you see San Francisco."

"I'm really anxious to meet your family."

We stopped in San Mateo to freshen up and put another sweater on Sambeau. The late afternoon was sunny with a chill. I threw Eric's flight jacket over my wrinkled sweater and skirt as we drove ahead.

"Everyone is at the Vallejo Street house tonight but we'll leave for Pebble Beach in a few days. They're really anxious to meet you and the baby and I'm glad it's light enough for you to see a little of the city. It's built on hills, like Rome--only better of course. And it belongs very much to this century which should be something different for you."

The three-storied house where we stopped overlooked a sweep of San Francisco Bay. Lights blinked below us and ships ruffled gray water of the Bay as they crossed under the high bridge before going on to the Pacific.

"Oh, Eric," I groped for a word, "It's all so--elegant."

He walked ahead of me through a wrought iron gate and pushed open the wide front door. A flurry of arms reached out and drew him inside the entrance hall into a circle of welcoming cries. A step behind him, I saw a small woman standing apart from the activity of the others, staring at me. She held a long cigarette holder she swept to her mouth. Her brown-gray hair was pulled tautly back from an angular face; the eyes frozen on me were unblinking slits. I thought of a bird of prey swaying on a tree branch. Although she was barely five feet tall, I felt she towered above me in her light blue dinner gown. I waited in the doorway in my skirt and sweater under the flight jacket, six inches taller than she, and felt like a willful child who wandered in from the cold night, eager for shelter. The glint behind thin lines of mascara spoke to me without words. Suddenly, her hands with long scarlet nails reached out. I stood breathless. She was going to welcome me, even show affection. I had misjudged her at the first shattering glance. She would embrace me now as a newcomer to the family, the vessel that put forth her grandchild, her continuity. Her hands lifted and swooped Sambeau from my arms without a word, turned and disappeared with him around a corner in the entrance hall.

Eric hugged his father who leaned heavily against him while he kept one hand on his shoulder and sheltered the drink he carried in the other.

A young blonde stood by the wall near the foyer entrance holding a half-finished martini in one hand. "Hi," she extended the other. "I'm Gwendolyn, Eric's sister. Welcome to San Francisco." She shook her short-cut sculptured head like a restless stallion and moved closer to Eric, her black crepe dinner slacks tight against slim hips. "All right, little brother, tell me everything. What are the English girls really like?" The three of them laughed and moved from the foyer to the living room.

A thin man in a gray suit with open collar came toward me and took the diaper bag. He didn't say anything, but looked at me with kind eyes.

He put his hand behind my waist and led me down the hall. "We'll find him. But remember this--and I had to learn it the hard way--don't say anything to Mr. Sorensen when he's this drunk. He slugs first and asks questions later. Nobody's safe."

"My baby. Find him please."

"Gladys--Mrs. Sorensen--is in the passing-out stage but they're down here somewhere. I was on the phone with a patient in the upstairs hall and I would have seen her walk by." He opened a door to a small den. Sambeau lay wide-awake on a leather couch, waving his hands and feet in the air. The spectre from the entrance hall sat beside him in a deep sleep, her mouth open.

Sometime before Frieda announced dinner, Eric remembered me. "Come on in, darling, and join us for a drink."

Gwendolyn sat opposite me at the large oblong dinner table with sounds of the city muffled by heavy draperies drawn for privacy. She talked to Eric about San Francisco gossip, her voice strident and husky from cigarettes she chainsmoked. Mrs. Sorensen had staggered in to dinner leaning on Doug, still silent, the dark narrow slits fixed on me without moving. Finally she spoke, calling out to her husband who sat at the opposite end of the table with his eyes half-closed.

"Her hair. Look at her hair. And her clothes. Gwendolyn, tomorrow, no later, you must take her to I.

Magnin's for something decent to wear." She lifted her drink, draining it while the jade cigarette holder bobbed in the yellow-stained fingers of her other hand. "My darling boy," I heard the trace of a mid-European accent as she lifted Eric's hand and kissed it. "This filthy war. Its destroyed so many lives. I will somehow make it up to you."

Doug, seated next to me, whispered, "She has no idea what she's saying."

My throat was too full to speak but I turned to him, "Why?"

"Her only son is no longer hers and tonight, for the first time, it became a reality."

Mrs. Sorensen rose from the table during dessert with Eric's help and left the room. She had not spoken to me in the three hours since we arrived.

I excused myself early to tend to Sambeau and pretended sleep when Eric came to bed, falling over a chair on the way.

"Cady, Cady, wake up."

I lay on my side staring into the darkness of the unfamiliar room.

"What is it, darling? You're crying."

I turned my head into the pillow. "You couldn't possibly understand. I was remembering how once an old cotton mill worker bought a brand new suit from Sears Roebuck to come to my mother's home to tell her his son was missing in action."

I agreed with the spectre. The Iraqi and Afghanistan problems had destroyed many lives; both civilian and military.

Sambeau woke me at first light. I held him with our faces pressed against the window, gray mist outside pressing back.

"That's fog," I told him. "Maybe later today when it's warmer you and I will walk in it together, taste it and push at it with our hands. Does ocean mist have a texture, do you think?" He was interested only in his bottle. "It runs in the Sorensen family, kiddo." We sat on the needlepoint-covered Queen Anne chair to see what the first rays of the sun would do to the moist white veil that hid San Francisco. Eric slept without stirring.

It was ten o'clock in Georgia. Mother would be sitting in the breakfast room having her mid-morning coffee, Dola at the kitchen table talking to her from the kitchen across fifteen feet of space, two aging women haunted by the same ghosts, bonded together across an impassable bridge.

After I settled Sambeau in his crib I looked in the Queen Anne desk drawer for writing paper.

"Dear Mother:

I hope you are reading this aloud to Dola. We arrived in San Francisco yesterday afternoon. It is a glamorous city in a way I have never seen before--sophisticated and arty. The fact is, it is many things I have never experienced before. What I really want to say is that I miss each of you terribly." I put down the pen and laid my head against the grain of wood on the desk top. I miss the oak trees and red clay banks at the end of our street and ivy climbing over the bricks in front of our house. I miss the smell of the cotton mill when the wind blows from the west and the scents of pine trees behind the garage when sun is heavy on their needles. I miss the Ocmulgee River. It is so old and has seen so much--the beauty of the past and the sadness that followed--like my family and like The Oaks when it was young. It was young, once, wasn't it? Wasn't I? Why did it all have to change?

But not everything had changed. Not Miss Eugenie and not Dola. They were a constant like the old brown river. I crumbled the paper and wiped tears from my face.

The bedroom door opened an inch or two, then wider. Mrs. Sorensen entered and stood at the foot of the bed, her gaunt hand with its fiery fingernails curled around the bedpost. Her smile was like the grimace of a painted whitewashed skull.

"I want you to call me 'Mummy'," she said.

# CHAPTER 17

Eric and I drove south to Pebble Beach with Sambeau asleep in his bassinet.

"We'll probably have a few people over tonight," Eric said, "friends I haven't seen in three or four years. Some of my old school buddies, friends of Mother's and Dad's. Be especially nice to Kenneth and Betsy O'Malley. I introduced them to each other while she and I were dating." We drove awhile in silence. "To tell you the truth, everyone--especially Mother and Dad--expected me to marry Betsy. She was supposed to have a huge debut at the Hillsborough Country Club before her father died and spoiled everything."

"Sounds interesting. You all will have a lot to celebrate tonight."

"Yeah, especially Kenneth. I mean, he never was able to join up. He couldn't get into any of the services because of his eyes."

I looked down at my sweater and jeans and wondered what dress Gwendolyn would choose for me to wear that night.

The house overlooking the golf course filled with people as the sun eased its way down behind a gray ocean. Eric found his way to Betsy O'Malley, a sleek brunette, and mingled with the crowd after cries of welcome quieted. Doug introduced me as each guest arrived. Stares rose from my black pumps to the white silk blouse above a black velvet skirt. Comments about my accent were harder to accept--a dozen "Georgia peaches", countless "honeychiles" and one "magnolia transplant". I liked Kenneth O'Malley at once, a soft-spoken young man with thick glasses. We fit into a niche of quiet conversation, finding unexpected connections to each other. He explained why Hemingway was his favorite American writer.

"Westerners are careful with words--we corral them, groom them, then use as few as possible."

"Southerners are the opposite," I said. "Words spill out of us like a newly opened bottle of champagne, flowing and golden and almost as unstoppable."

"The twain have met." We touched glasses.

I knew this group gathered frequently, whether in San Francisco or down the coast. The cheek-pressings, blending with "darlings" and "divines", began in a low, bored register. By the third drink, the sound decible soared.


Then the arguments started comparing WWII with the Iraqi and Afghanistan situations.

"Isn't it divine? No blackouts," some woman said. "The government won't be taking my good Japanese help away like they did during the big War."

"My mother told me her garden went to seed the day our yardman Oshida had to leave," another said. "She felt angry, but . . ."

"Well, better times ahead."

"This war is another Vietnam," one of the men pipped in.

Doug sat at the grand piano and played Noel Coward tunes.

"Darling, play something from that marvelous 'Carousel' score." While everyone began singing "June Is Busting Out All Over", I slipped out to check on Sambeau. I turned a corner in the dark hallway and saw Eric and Betsy holding each other, kissing deeply. The thick carpet silenced my steps as I returned to the living room and leaned against a bookcase, seeing letters on the brightly covered best sellers without understanding any words. I looked out over the chic women with their tennis-tanned husbands--pampered glamour mated with bored suavity. My homesickness hit like a horse's kick in my stomach.

Doug's voice came through to me. "The club for dinner, I'll call ahead."

"Not that dull place. Besides, after these hors d'hourves who could eat anything. Fabulous, darling."

"Gladys has artistry dripping from her fingers. Or were they catered, you sly mouse?"

Gladys swayed slightly in the middle of the room holding Sambeau in her arms. Doug and I jumped to flank her.

"Oh, Nels, it's you in miniature!"

"Marvelous baby."

"'Minnesota' must be the Indian word for 'gorgeous men'."

I put Sambeau back in his basinet. "You are gorgeous, darling, in any language, but I want you to be so many other things besides."

I stayed behind with him while the others left for dinner at the Club and sent the Mexican housekeeper off to bed when the food and glasses were cleared. The long living room shone with heavy mahagony and red velvet furniture which the Sorensens collected from old Spanish missions along the California coast or in antique galleries around Carmel. I felt myself drawn to the one ugly object in the room --a stuffed cougar on top of a low Mission table against a wall. His yellow teeth snarled beneath a perpetual glare while he crouched in an attack position, one paw lifted with nails bared.

"You're too late, honey," I patted his brown head. "There's nothing left on my bones tonight. But take heart- -Southern women are good at shaking off the dust of ashes and snapping back to life."

I heard the Sorensen's car drive in before eleven. When I greeted them,Eric and Gwendolyn half-carried their mother to the master bedroom; Doug closed the door to the small study probably to call the hospital in San Francisco about a patient. Mr. Sorensen drew me into the kitchen.

"I want to show you the secret of my world-famous martinis -- Beef-eater gin only and rinse each utensil five times to get rid of any trace of soap."

I stood beside him at a counter while he prepared another pitcher-full. Without warning, he swung me around to face him and forced his tongue into my mouth as he kissed me.

"No, please." I pulled away and ran from the kitchen.

"What the hell is the matter with you?" Eric stood in the door of our room. Lying in bed in darkness even at a distance I knew he was drunk.

"The baby is asleep," I whispered.

He turned on the bedside lamp. "You've been unfriendly and rude all evening. I know you. I saw you sneering at our friends, too damn superior to join us for dinner." He stood before me.

"You're drunk, Eric, like your father."

He came closer and pulled me from the bed to a standing position. "And what was your father like, sugarbelle? Did he start from scratch on a farm in Minnesota and build an empire like this for his family? I've seen that rundown hundred-year-old wreck of a house in Georgia hanging by a nail. Any minute it could crash down on the head of that crazy mother of yours who acts like she's Queen Elizabeth."

He had pushed me back to a closet and with his hands on my shoulders banged my head against the door punctuating each sentence.

Not raising my voice, I whispered, "You poor dumb fool."

"Don't you ever call me a fool again." His slap across my face brought tears to my eyes. "None of my family likes you--they know you married me for my money."

His hands slipped up to my throat and circled it.

"Look around you, honeybelle. We have everything, everything anybody could want."

"No," I was barely able to speak as his hands tightened. "There's one thing not one of you can ever have."

"What?" He banged my head against the door harder as his thumbs met and pressed against my throat. "Tell me. What can't we ever have?"

Somewhere in the blackness that hovered in auras around my head, during flashes of sound like bells striking my brain, a word came to me that I had never spoken, had never heard spoken, but in my last moment of consciousness gave birth to from some unknown parentage. "Class," I whispered before I slid to the floor.

# CHAPTER 18

"Cady, my darling. I'm so sorry." Eric's shoulders heaved as he dug his head into the space between my arm and left breast. "Sweetheart, forgive me." His tears flowed down my chest, wetting the sheet. "I guess I just went ape last night from being home and all the martinis. Forgive me, please forgive me."

Sambeau cried in his basinet. I reached for my robe and held him close to me. He looked like a baby food advertisement with his blond hair and eyes bluer than a Minnesota lake. What had made this baby? Animal passion? Desolation calling out to desperation?

I rocked him against my shoulder and walked over to the wide window. Pebble Beach had less fog than San

Francisco and I watched Seventeen Mile Drive shed mists of the night.

A stranger in a stranger land. Had my ancestor who stepped ashore on Virginia's beach over 300 years ago felt as alienated from his past as I did now? Almost the same distance separated me from my home and culture. I ached for the gracious, time-resisting land that knows change is pushing and prodding at its borders, but with its particular politesse, bids it a gentle welcome.

Gwendolyn brought her morning coffee into our bedroom and sat at the foot of the bed.

"You can bet your sweet ass that will be the last martini I ever drink," she said in her hoarse voice to Eric who lay nude under the covers. "How about you, sweetie?" She turned her short cropped head toward me. "You must have been downing them like a thirsty sailor."

"I had one and a half," I said.

"Fat chance. You look like holy hell. Go look in the mirror and then tell me you had only two drinks last night."

"She tripped in the dark and hit her head against the bedpost," Eric spoke quickly.

"Her face is as puffy as a blowfish. You, Eric, had better get your tail out of bed and into the shower. We're all due at the Armstrong wedding at noon." Her eyes ran up and down me like amber spiders. The dressing gown I wore had been made two years ago by Miss Lula, our colored seamstress and friend, especially for my trousseau. Until this moment I thought the pastel polished cotton was beautiful-- now I felt like a blowfish in a tacky homemade bathrobe.

"You'll want to stay home with the baby," Gwendolyn said. "But you," she jiggled Eric's foot, "get moving."

After the others left for the wedding, I roamed around the lovely Spanish villa with Sambeau on one arm. The main house stood on a hill, built with two levels; front picture windows of each faced the ocean. As I turned the corner of the house to an open grassed area in back, spaced with lawn furniture and a barbecue pit, I heard familiar sounds coming from the drive winding deep into cypress trees. Two or three horses stamped and snorted and I smelled hay and leather. Oh, dear God, no, not a stable.

I ran to the front of the house. A strange coast line stretched before me. Large gray boulders hovered close to the beach. The ocean smelled cold and trees leaned away from it like cringing, beaten prisoners. It was theatrical, a surreal landscape. I stood and stared in the biting air. It was not salt water and sea wind I smelled. It was new money.

# CHAPTER 19

Eric received orders for temporary shore duty at Alameda across the Bay in Oakland. He had injured his back and the Navy doctors grounded him. The Sorensens insisted we stay with them while we looked for a house to rent or buy.

"I'd like to take a couple of days leave and show you the Big Sur," he said while I was packing to leave Pebble Beach. "It's worth seeing and we need some time alone."

"Sambeau?"

"Mother--and Frieda, of course," he added quickly, "could take care of him. Gwen and Doug would keep an eye on things. Come on, baby. There are trees down there that will make you think Georgia pines are match sticks.

This is my home state and I want you to see more of it. Big Sur is spectacular."

It was. Heavy thought drifted away on the scent of redwood trees. We walked deep into the forest the first afternoon and lay beneath a two hundred foot feathery green redwood that moaned gently around us.

"Why are you smiling?" Eric said later as I rested my face against his shoulder.

"I was remembering walking together in Biscayne Park under those funny, rattling palm trees. Everything there was so different. Remember waves hitting the sea walls and the smell of salt water?"

Northern California was crisp, sharp and distinctive. Earlier in the day we had climbed to a restaurant like an aerie on a hill high above the Pacific.

"The air, sunlight and the water gleam and glow," I'd said, "It's as if they were regulated, following orders to be absolutely perfect-- without a flaw." We listened now to the sway of the limbs spreading above us. "If you all could just let me live easy-like, not perfect, not orderly with spit and polish. Please let me be me, Eric."

His arms lay across his closed eyes. "I'm trying, Cady."

"I know. I don't think either one of us had any idea how completely different we are."

"No. We didn't. And I know Mother and Gwen haven't been all that nice to you. But they've never met anyone from the Deep South before. You're different from any of the girls I used to date."

"I'm not a glamour queen, you mean. Well, being a sleek 'socialite' was never one of my ambitions." I sat up and put my head against my knees. "I come from defeated people who live in a once-defeated State. Somehow my family never really snapped back. I don't know why we didn't. It must seem strange to you all."

"You could try to be a little more . . ." He groped for a word.

"Sophisticated? Worldly and glib like Betsy?" I asked.

"Well, Mother has always loved Betsy."

After a minute I said, "Please hold me, Eric. I don't feel lonely when you hold me."

Rhythms of the forest circled us again. Walking back later to The Lodge House where we were staying I looked around at the foot-loose summer season of Big Sur. Bears and cougars lived there in peace with their differentness. Couldn't we forget ours? After dinner we sat on a small ledge around a large fireplace with other tourists in The Lodge House listening to conversation rise and quicken over the Iraqi situation. "We could be there for the next ten years," a man said.

Back in San Francisco I searched for Miss Eugenie's distinctive handwriting in the daily mail delivery on the entrance hall table. Her letters made tactful comments on the fascinating differences in our large country--as diverse in many ways as Europe but bound by the same ideal that linked each part to the others. The pages of black ink in her finishing-school round handwriting became vitamin shots, revitalizing me for another day.

"How is your mother?" Gwendolyn asked once.

I shook my head. "It's hard to tell with her."

"Wow!" Eric shouted one Saturday afternoon in early August while we all looked over the mail together after lunch on the terrace with several Bloody Marys. "Look, Mother. Take a quick glance at this little item." He held a square cream-colored envelope in the air and waved it above his head. "An invitation for Commander and Mrs. Eric Sorensen to attend the San Francisco Opera Ball in October."

"Let me see." Gwendolyn and Gladys each reached for it.

"Can you believe this? Cady and I are invited to the Opera Ball." He picked his mother up by the waist and swung her around in a circle while Gwendolyn scanned the engraved words. "We're on our way. This is the real thing," he said.

"Real what?" I asked.

"Top San Francisco society." He pulled me up the stairs to our room. "Mother and Dad, even Gwen and Doug, have wanted this for years. How do you suppose this happened and why now? The O'Malleys have gone to it every year but this is the first time for my family."

"Miss Eugenie graduated in music--she knows opera-lovers all over the country. Maybe ..."

"Oh, no, don't try to convince me your mother had anything to do with this, living like a crazy hermit in that old relic of a house. No, it had nothing to do with her, I'm sure."

I tried to remember how many Bloody Marys he'd had for lunch. "I really don't know," I said. "Perhaps she is eccentric but she's never rude."

"And who are you calling rude? My mother?" He grabbed my shoulders with rough hands.

I pushed him away. "Don't go on like this, Eric. I don't want to begin resenting you."

"Are you sure it's not too late for that?"

"I care very much about you."

"Like hell. I was a goddam port in a storm. All of my family says that."

"Then they're mistaken. If I used you in any way, it wasn't intentional. Look back. Remember some things--I gave you the most I had to give at the time."

He turned from the window to face me. "All you Southern girls are hot tomatoes, ripe for fucking. Well, you've cooled off some, Sugarbelle."

"Fever-pitch feelings can't last forever, Eric. Everything changes with time." I wished that was true.

"Yeah. It sure does, babe!"

Frieda knocked on the door. "There's a telephone call for you, Miss, from Georgia. You wish to take it in the upstairs hall or in the den?"

I jumped down the stairs two at a time and shut the door of the small room behind me.

"Is that you, baby?" the connection crackled.

"Dola! Dola, how is my mother?"

"She ain't so good. Maybe you could slip on home for a spell. Miss Aggie she done told me how to call you and to say you should come on back for awhile. How is you, baby?"

"I have a lot to tell you."

"I bet it ain't going to be no surprise to me."


"Just take care of everything until Sambeau and I get there."

Upstairs Eric stood in the middle of the bedroom. "But what about the Opera Ball? You can't leave now."

"My mother's need against that silly party? Guess which one I'll choose."

"This is something my family has wanted for years. You could go home later. There's no emergency."

"Take Betsy O'Malley to the Opera Ball. That would please everybody except her poor, innocent, cuckolded husband."

He stared at me from a face frozen with surprise.

"Sit down, Eric. I want to explain something to you. There's no such thing in San Francisco as 'society', unless you happen to belong to one of the families of very old Spanish descent and I don't think you all know anyone who does."

"What do you mean, no society here?" he stood up. "Kenneth's great-grandfather owned the Northern American Railroad."

"Kenneth is a nice man. I like him. He deserves better than Betsy. You're making me into a snob, Eric. I never thought about these things until I ran into your absurd, pretentious people out here. It's ridiculous."

"You're as crazy as the rest of your screwed-up family."

"You're probably right. What's so terribly, earth-shatteringly important to you all doesn't mean a fig to us."

He glared at me. "You are a bitch," he said quietly.

"I'm what life forces me to be, because I'm going to survive, Eric, with or without you."

"Make it without." He left the room and softly closed the door behind him.

On the Delta flight to Atlanta the Captain of the plane announced that turbulence was ahead. The seat belt sign was turned on. I picked up Sambeau and held him tightly on my lap. He choked on the sip of champagne I was having. It brought tears to his eyes. I did not try to explain mine but let them run down my face undisturbed.

# CHAPTER 20

Dola and I sat at the kitchen table after I settled Sambeau in the crib that Emory, Claudia and I had used as children.

She patted my hand. "You mama ain't well enough to hear 'bout you breaking up your marriage yet awhile--her being so thick with them nuns and all."

I nodded my head. "But wait a minute. I heard there's a great doctor in Atlanta, a specialist in--her condition." The word I could not say had been tabu, in limbo, for too many centuries.

"Forget them doctors." Her hand covered mine and lay still. "She been bleeding away inside since your Daddy died. Now she 'bout bleed herself out. When it's time, we gots to let her go."

Miss Eugenie rallied the week after Sambeau and I came home.

"Praise sweet God in the skies," Dola said one late August morning while she fixed a tray to take upstairs. "She wants a soft-boiled egg!"

Every one of my senses tingled to the particular treasure-house of Georgia. I lay in bed late each morning while sounds of my childhood rode in the window on waves of soft familiar languor. The vegetable man approached on his wagon, his progress down the street marked by barking of the neighbors' dogs. He stopped at each house--then clucked, jiggled the reins and led the creaking wagon to the next place. Only the neighborhood cooks understood his sing-song chant. I waited for the one recognizable phrase "roast-near corn"--that fell to a low note to end the melody. His voice dropped to an undertone in front of our house while he and Dola spoke their daily ritual through murmurs of easy laughter.

After nine o'clock Dola's hymns rose from the kitchen - African rhythms that pounded with Hardshell Baptist words mingled with clattering pans and an occasional curse. At ten o'clock Miss Agatha drove up in her gray Buick with a hamper of light delicate food-- finger paper thin chicken sandwiches, marinated artichoke hearts and small flaky apple tarts, books under one arm and more unasked for medical advice.

Who was I to say which one was successful. Miss Eugenie, fully dressed, walked downstairs one morning during the first week in September.

"How lovely everything is," she said although a layer of dust tinted each piece of furniture. "Autumn is such a haunting time of the year, isn't it? I smell burning leaves-- delicious, but a little sad, don't you all agree? Endings are, you know, except in the Near East. We must pray to God for the safe return of our brave men in uniform there."

"Yes'm. But you sure you ain't smelling burned toast and bacon? Miss Cady been cooking today while I ease my bones."

"Cady, darling, you actually can cook? I guess we needed an influx of new red blood in our veins and obviously the Sorensens provided it."

"They provided a lot more in my blood than you will ever know."

Miss Eugenie gave me her look that meant I was approaching bad taste.

"Well, their genes certainly gave you a beautiful child."

Mother wore a touch of rouge on her face and I felt giddy--the heavy weight on my spirit like a blanket of stone lifted. As we moved to the breakfast room I asked her if she felt up to a little gossip.

One hand touched the chignon at the back of her long neck. "Gossip? About whom?"

"Well, name anybody. Dola has given me the scoop on all the people this side of the Mississippi."

"Sure has. Us coloreds hear words coming through the air better than Western Union." While she cleared the table she said, "These eggs was good. This whole breakfast good. I's proud of you, baby--I raised you fine."

"My two chicks who fled the nest turned out well, don't you think so, Dola?" Mother and I stayed in our chairs enjoying the path of autumn through the oak trees beyond the windows in back of our house.

"One done fly back, praise God."

"Was there something you wanted to tell me, Cady?"

"Yes, Mother." I put down my coffee cup. "Eric and I are separated."

She sat across the breakfast table, paler than before, rouge standing out in clear marks on her cheeks.

"There has never been a divorce in our family. Ever."

"Well, I'm afraid there's going to be one soon. I think both sides should be delighted."

Three weeks after Sambeau and I came back to Georgia a letter from Gwendolyn arrived. I was badly missed and when was I coming "home"? Eric was like a rudderless ship and the house seemed dreadfully empty without the baby. Even Frieda said that my Southern accent was the most beautiful way of speaking next to German.

I found a piece of my old bridal note paper from J.P. Stevens Engravers, Atlanta, and answered that perhaps Eric and I married too hastily when we both suddenly discovered we knew very little about each other. I added that Eric must feel free to visit us at any time in our very old house that was held together by one very strong nail. I wrote that it would still be standing long after we were gone. It needed a coat of paint, of course. I needed a coat of paint as her family so graciously pointed out, but what was lacking in our marriage was that it was all shiny new paint over no substance. I mailed the letter the same afternoon.

Eric called the next week to ask if I was ready to stop acting like a horse's ass and could he visit on his next leave.

"Of course," I said. "Anytime. As one says in real California society, 'Mi casa es tu casa.'"

He hung up.

It surprised me to see Miss Eugenie become good friends with Sambeau. I did not remember her holding me on her láp in a rocking chair and singing old plantation songs. One about a Kentucky bird who flew away to rest closed my throat and sent me from the room in tears.

"Please don't ever sing that one again," I begged her.

"Cady, you should cherish every memory of your father and not push them away."

"Mother, one of the signposts on my very private path says 'Don't Look Back at the Wrong Things'. I can't live in sadness."

She continued to sing to Sambeau in her light high-pitched voice about a big Alabama moon shining round and yellow to watch the cotton fields grow whiter.

"I don't think that would play too well in Pebble Beach," I whispered to Dola.

"Now you hush your mouth and let your mama be."

# CHAPTER 21

The morning started out wrong. Sambeau woke up fretful when I bent over his crib. "You look like Peter Rabbit with those two red eyes," I said.

I leaned over the stairwell and asked Dola to come upstairs to look at him.

"He got pink-eye," she said.

In the middle of the morning I told her I was going to call Dr. Happ.

"Don't waste no money on no doctor. Go to the drug store, get some borum acid."

"Boric acid and water, of course. I remember Miss Eugenie putting something cool in my eyes when I was very little."

"Miss Genie ain't put nothing in you nowhere, no time. I's the one take care of you when you was little bitty."

"Thank you, dear saint. I think I need the walk to the drug store." Miss Eugenie napped upstairs and Sambeau kept his fists against his eyes. "Will you just stay healthy until I get back?" I asked Dola.

"I ain't never been healthy. Had misery bones all my life."

"Please try to stay alive for a few more minutes. I'll bring you back some vanilla ice cream."

"Then take the car. I don't want no vanilla juice."

Pearsons Drug Store held the story of my life. I had roamed its sweet-smelling aisles with Eula Belle when we were children and twirled on counter stools while Mr. Pearson served us orange popsicles. Later, I ordered chocolate shakes on Saturday afternoons and flirted with Lanier High School boys. We all blushed at the displays of sanitary napkins. Now I sat at one of the small tables with a Coke to wait while Mr Pearson tried to remember where he kept cans of boric acid. Berkley Hollingsworth sat at the far end of the counter having a cup of coffee.

"Well," he moved closer. "if it's not Mrs. Olaf Svensenborg, or something unpronounceable like that. Are you divorced yet or is it still pending?"

"Berkley, since we are such old, dear friends, I want you to feel free to ask me rude personal questions whenever you like. Don't bother with manners--just spit it out as you always have."

"It so happens I already know," he said. "My mother talks to Miss Eugenie twice a day on the phone."

"How nice."

"Well, I can see the loss of your virginity certainly didn't make you any sweeter. Pity. By the way, your old friend is back, you know."

"What old friend?"

"I forget his name. The mill boy, the one who worked for your family and the newspaper made so much of his being missing in action." I looked down at my Coke and twirled ice with the straw. In my mind I saw Willie's coffin being taken off a troop ship to send to his parents for burial. Southerners belong to their land, and repay the lush senuousness of their lives by giving themselves to the red clay in death.

But how would Berkley know about Willie's coffin?

"You didn't hear me." Berkley's voice came from somewhere in a distance.

I lifted my eyes to look at him.


"The chopper he was riding aboard as a passenger exploded in flames, but the rear rotor section broke free and landed in some trees. He was seriously injured with a few others, but survived okay. It seems he and the other survivors had to hide out for a long time." Berkley shrugged. "Anyway, he came down to Macon looking for you. I happened to spot him filling up his SUV while I was gassing my wagon; went over to say hello. I told him, of course, you married a Yankee and had a son."

It took a moment for my brain to begin functioning again. I leapt out of the metal drug store chair and threw my arms around him.

"I love you, Berkley. I adore you, you miserable bastard," I said. I whirled out of the pharmacy and ran back to the car where I sobbed against the steering wheel.

An older woman on the sidewalk stopped and leaned in the window on the other side of the front seat.

"Are you feeling all right, Miss? Can I he'p you any?"

I raised my head. "He's alive," I told her. "Willie is alive."

"Oh, precious, that's so fine. Whoever he is, I'm real proud for you. You be happy now, you hear?"

I threw myself into Dola's arms when I ran in the back door sobbing. "I forgot your vanilla ice cream."

"Jesus. It don't matter that much."

"Dola," I clung to her. "Willie's alive. Berkley Hollingsworth just told me so in the drug store."

"Come on over here and set down with me." She led me to the table. "I heard talk about it but I couldn't say nothing 'til I was sure. Couldn't make you go through no more sadness if it wasn't true, you having it so bad with that old devil-woman out yonder in the West." She rubbed my shoulders and brought me a box of Kleenex. "Miss Eugenie had a day nurse one week mumbled something to me 'bout some man come by here looking for you, but

I didn't pay her no mind. I was at my Lodge meeting so must have been on a Thursday afternoon. The nurse tell him ain't nobody young live here no more."

"Berkley saw him and talked to him so he wasn't a ghost. And I've read and reread Miss Eugenie's letters about his plane crash. They said some remains were found which means others got out. Oh, Dola, did anyone ever tell you that you are a beautiful, gorgeous woman?"

"Nobody sober with the lights on."

"I wonder where he is?"

"Don't fret. He find you, wait and see."

But he won't. He thinks I am happily married somewhere in the North living the good life with my husband and child.

The September night was cool, and I shivered on grass under the biggest of the oak trees. Light on yellowing leaves above me was from a large, gentle moon, touching Georgia fields where sugar cane, pumpkins and gourds turned golden under its fullness. Somewhere it was touching him. Let him be happy, God, wherever he is.

Two hours later I awoke from a heavy sleep and jumped up. Sambeau. Upstairs alone while Miss Eugenie slept her drugged slumber. I ran to lean over his bed and feel his forehead. Cool. Tomorrow I'd ask Dola to help me move our things into Emory's room so I could look out of the window at the back lawn and my old playhouse. Willie's garden in front of it went to seed years ago but Sambeau and I would pull out the weeds and make it thrive again. Some things were out and out meant to last forever.

# CHAPTER 22

Seasons moved again into green, gold, red, brown, then empty gray branches, groping and touching while they watched time slide by year after year, practicing their secret sign language to each other through the changes.

"I bet you'll like kindergarten better this year," I told Sambeau while he showed Dola his new brown oxfords for the third time one morning. "Don't you think so?"

"No," he said.

"And before long you'll be able to write letters to your new half-brother in California. Will you like that?"

"No."

Dola rocked him in her lap. "That new half-brother and him got something in common. Both got a half-ass for a father."

"It was long ago and far away." I told her. I thought of one of the songs Eric and I moved to at the 79th Street Causeway restaurant in Miami where youth and life itself begged us to be part of the dance.

Miss Eugenie looked pale when she came downstairs later than usual but at lunch she turned to me with some of her old vivacity.

"Cady, please be kind enough to help me out this afternoon. One of the nuns needs to be driven up to Forsythe. Her brother's been hurt in a tractor accident-- not badly, but injured nevertheless, and I promised you would take her home for a visit."

"Of course. You know I'm not so good at directions but maybe she'll know the way."

"Of course she will. She grew up there."

The countryside rose as Sister Loyola and I drove north on the Atlanta Highway. The Appalachian chain lifted us as hills became fullgrown blue-tinted mountains waiting like courtly old gentlemen to rise and bid me welcome. At every curve my childhood washed over me-- summer at camp in Clayton, or in our white clapboard house in Saluda, North Carolina. The years were like a string of prayer beads, each stone to be touched and fondled before lingering fingers moved on to another and another.

Strident tones of rural Georgia speech finally reached me as we came to the outskirts of Forsythe. "That's new," Sister Loyola said and pointed to a Bar-b-que stand where a group of black people stood talking near the side of the road. A school building rose on the left and their children hovered around playground swings like circling birds waiting to light. "I never saw that before." she said.

"Nothing stays the same, Sister. Remember St Teresa's prayer, `God alone is changeless'."

"That's true. But some of the changes here are coming too fast for me." She fanned her pink face with a large white handkerchief. "The big War brought so many things down here to us. I wish we could go back to the old ways and days."

"Well, we both know we won't ever do that." I stopped before a crossroads traffic light. "I think we're near the city limits now. Which way do I turn?"

"Why, everything is so different around here with all these new buildings springing up everywhere," Sister said. "Let's find somebody to ask how to get to Jenkins Grocery Store. That's where my family buys things."

I turned right, then drove deeper into the woods, a few houses thinning out to none. The sun lowered in the sky. "Is any of this familiar to you at all?"

"Why no, it isn't." I heard a whisper of fear in her voice. "This is not the direction I would have turned. Let's go back the other way."


I drove a half mile farther down the road and saw a lean-to house back in the woods across a patch of yellow grass, listless as August. When I pulled off the narrowing lane and stopped the engine I noticed a wisp of smoke from a lone brick chimney inching its way into the sky.

"That house is certainly old enough for the people living there to know what's what around here," I said.

"Wait!" she cried. "What if they're . . ."

"They are what?"

"You know. Nigras."

"They'll know the way to the grocery store, Sister Loyola. They eat, too, believe it or not."

Her round blue eyes glittered behind rimless glasses.

"They also do other things. Unspeakable things, especiallly to white women like you and me."

"Let's chance it," I said. "I'll ask them for directions."

Her hand clutched me until my arm ached.


"Now you listen here. You're not going to leave me all alone in the car, Cady Worthington. You got us lost in this shanty country. You've driven us to the gates of Hades out here with these mean-eyed nigra people with those purple beards about to pop out on their faces. Have you ever noticed a nigra man has blue-purple skin when he needs a shave?"

"I never noticed that."

She was right--we were lost. This car was hellbound but I did not do it.

The dog that greeted me on the steps of the planked front porch was almost as tall as I when he stood on his hind legs with his paws on my shoulders. "Thanks," I pulled his ears. "That's what I've been needing badly--kisses and more kisses--loads of kisses all over my face."

"Would you help me, please?" I said to the gray haired black man who opened the door. "I have a nun in the car back there and we're lost. We're looking for the Mulcahy farm which is about a mile from Jenkins Grocery Store."

"Sure can. You goes . . .", he turned to point over a forest of pines. "Missy, it too hard to tell you. Let me just ride and take you there, then I'll cut home through the woods."

"I don't want to trouble you."

He lowered his head and shuffled his feet. "Ain't no trouble. Nobody here but me and Daniel," he pointed to the dog.

"I wish we could take him along for the ride but the other passenger is sort of nervous. I'm not sure she likes dogs."

"Rest your mind."

As I opened the door to the back seat I said to him, "I'm afraid I don't know your name."

"Fisher, ma'am. Folks just calls me Fisher."

"Mr. Fisher, this is Sister Loyola from Macon here to visit her family."

Her gasp was audible as she stared straight ahead. From the back seat, Fisher directed me down the stretch of baked clay road and pointed to a cluster of roofs I saw ahead through a copse of deepening elms and maples. "Right yonder is Jenkins place. I walks it myself once a week or so."

"Is there a service station near here?"

"Sure is. Round this corner like."

After the gas tank was filled I saw I had no cash in my purse, only a check book. Mrs. Worthington Sorensen had a small bank balance but no identity in Forsythe, Georgia.

"Sister Loyola, do you have any cash?" I asked her. "I'll pay you back later when we get to Macon."

She sat on the edge of the front seat grasping the door handle, staring ahead with her face frozen.

"I has ten dollars," Fisher said. "I cut kindling all last week and I can spare easy what you need."

"You've been so kind already but we really are helpless."

"Ain't no trouble a'tall. Just mail it to me when you can, care of Jenkins Store."

"I promise you I will. Thank you, Mr. Fisher, for lending us four dollars and for your kindness to us."

He lifted his hat and stared down at his feet again before turning to walk back down the dusty road.

A woman clerk at the grocery store gave us directions to Mulcahy's farm. When we stopped at the neat, white house with the last rays of sun drawing away from its clipped orderly fields, I held my hand across the seat with the palm upward. "I'll pay half. You owe me two bucks," I said. "Sister."

A cold mist hung over Macon in the middle of September.

"We gots to find somebody to take care of them fireplaces. Joe Henry done been spoiled doing that other kind of work and it's getting harder and harder to get him to help us out 'round here."

"Yes, the times they are a'changing. But listen," I said. "I met a really nice man in Forsythe with a wonderful dog named Daniel."

"Like in the lion's den?"

"Probably, yes. They could live here in the playhouse. His name is Fisher and he's sort of old but he could stir up the fires and clean the grates."

"How old?"

"What did you have in mind, Dola? He's still young enough to lay a fire."

"I knows where your ugly mind is going. I was wondering is all."

"We could drive up and talk to him."

"He may be has roots there. Rooted to his land. Some is, some ain't. Does he grow things?"

"There were some ferns on the front porch and a hydrangia bush by the steps."

"Don't talk foolishness. I mean the land. Do the land give him food? Cause if it do, if the land done give him life, he ain't go budge from it no way 'till the angels come to fetch him."

# CHAPTER 23

On Wednesday morning I awoke with the blankets on the floor and Indian summer shining outside the windows.

"This air tastes like champagne," Miss Eugenie said at breakfast. "It actually tingles."

"Delicious," I agreed. I picked up Sambeau from kindergarten and admired the purple cat with orange eyes he had colored for Dola. I told him his talent deserved a special treat.

In the middle of the afternoon we came home from the wading pool Miss Pridey had put in for her grandnieces when they visited. Dola sat in her rocking chair in the kitchen, like an excited Buddah, quivering.

"I got some news," she said.

I settled a towel around Sambeau's shoulders.

"Emory's married, I bet. Who is she, the poor little idiot."

"That ain't it."

I poured lemonade for the three of us and brought the brown bottle from under the sink for Dola. "Okay. Let's have it." I sat in a straight kitchen chair turned backwards.

Her eyes glittered under the squares of plaited hair now gray in front. "I got a phone call today from a old friend."

My heart jumped all over my chest?

"He ask all 'bout you folks, specially 'bout you. I told him you was split up from your husband who was a prize bastard. I told Mr. Willie lots of things."

I could not breathe.

"He say he in Atlanta on business. Going to fly down here to Macon. Say he be at the Dempsey Hotel 'bout two hours from now."

On my knees beside her, I grabbed her arms with my hands.

"Child, you hurting me. I done fix it up for you two to meet for supper at 6:00 o'clock this evening.

Oh God Oh God Oh God!

"Sambeau!"

"Sambeau, stay here with me. I spend the night if I has to. Lots of room. Too much room."

Oh sweet dearest Jesus, thank You.

To Dola I said, "I'll be your slave for the rest of my life."

"That'll be a switch!"


All during my drive to downtown Macon I planned to be dignified, my trembling would stop and I'd behave as a sophisticated matron meeting an old friend. I parked my car on a side street and walked in the back entrance of the Dempsey to see him first and approach him with composure. He had left Macon a tall lanky country boy of twenty-three with a hick accent.

I saw his profile. He stood at a newspaper rack looking out onto Cherry Street. Willie. I thought I whispered it but he swung around and met me in the middle of the lobby. Minutes later we stopped holding each other long enough to pull apart and see each other's faces. He touched my hair with his left hand. The same startling blue eyes under black eyebrows.

"I have a room," he said.

I nodded.

We cradled each other, rocking back and forth, sometimes joined in love-making, sometimes lying quietly breathing in each other's scent. There were no words, only gentling sounds and occasional cries of disbelief, then the overwhelming realization that what was happening was true.

He pushed up to look at the length of me. "Cady. My beautiful lady." He gave me his slight easy smile, scar tissue on my mind that would never heal.

Then he said things I drank in like someone who falls into an oasis pool after a staggering walk through a desert. My thirst seemed endless. I kept my arms wrapped around his back, healing my dry barren fingers with the feel of him.

I walked in the front door of The Oaks late the next afternoon and crept to the kitchen.

Sambeau sat on Dola's lap feeding himself spoonsful of red Jello. "Jesus!" Dola said. "You shining like the harvest moon. Don't let your mama see your face. She'd know I been fibbing."

I covered Sambeau with kisses. "Dola, let me make you some special tea."

"That make sense. I ain't had none since you been gone, seeing as how I had this child to watch out for, so make it strong. Your mama think it real strange you had to leave home so fast. I told her one of your friends from that school in Florida wanted you to meet her in Atlanta." She sighed. "I hates lying to Miss Genie. She so dumb it just don't seem right."

"Dola, Willie has a cabin in Tennessee where he goes fishing. He wants me to spend some time with him up there. What do you think?"

"I think if your mama find out all hell break loose."

"I have something else to tell you. He was once sort of married."

She put down the tea. "How do somebody be sort of married?"

"Well, it's a strange situation--really hard to explain."

"Try."

"Willie felt obligated to the Iraqi family who saved his life. When they found him and the two other survivors, he suffered from a broken right shoulder and arm. Fortunately, the head of the house was a doctor. The family kept them hidden from what they call insurgents. Willie hears the family has relatives in the states and wants to send their daughter to New York where they live to get her out of the war zone. When found by the U.S. forces, Willie knew he would be sent home. He offered to marry the daughter so she could get out of the country. They forged a marriage certificate and pre-dated it to two years before the invasion."

I looked down at my hands clasped in my lap.

"When the Marines finally found Willie and his companions, their broken bodies had almost healed. Willie later found out that Marja had been able to obtain a passport and had safely arrived in New York."

Dola reached across the table and patted my arm.

I took a big gulp of my special tea. "He told me nothing was real but the four walls that hid them and the arid desert he saw from the window of the room. He knew I thought he was dead and I did, you know. Anyway, they're divorced in Iraqi courts now."


"Aw right, baby. Don't fret your mind. The good Lord in Heaven don't care 'bout no rules, what He studies is cases and your case be different. Real different. Go on up to Tennessee and roll around with Mr. Willie 'til you is black and blue."

I told her we would tell Miss Eugenie I was going to meet a group of friends again from St. Catherine. I promised to call home every day from the nearest town to check on everyone.

Before I left, she said, "If'n I'm going to all this trouble telling all them lies again, you two best be up there having yourselves a time, you hear?"

"You are an absolute angel," I said.

"No, I ain't. Angels is white."

"Who said so?"

"I seen them in picture books."

"Screw picture books."

"You just out and out ain't no lady."

"That's right. You speak the absolute truth." I threw her a kiss. "You two have fun."

"Jesus. Guess there ain't no need to say that to you!"


Willie met my plane in Chattanooga and we drove into the mountains to a cabin near a small lake fed by a stream pouring over flat gray stones. Inside we stopped before a fireplace flanked by two large wooden baskets he had filled with red and yellow leaves, mixed with wild asters and sumac berries. I knew that for the rest of my life, autumn would mean the warmth of rich colors and the gentleness of late afternoon sun waiting at western windows, touching my blood with the surety of finest wine.

Nights fled by us like streams breaking away from a long frozen winter, deep and throaty with woods sounds. Cicadas pounded a heady background to our love. In the mornings our hands reached for the first touch before we were really awake. Days were a feast of the senses--

goldenrod flaunting its color, the smell of burning logs, our pulses catching flame by low firelight.

The last afternoon we had a fish-fry around a curve in the lake where Willie said he was sure human life began.

"The first fish to flop up on dry land looked around at these hills and said 'Hey, I think we've got something here'."

"He was right, wasn't he?" I spread a plaid blanket on dried weeds at the shoreline and watched Willie cast his line in one fling into deep blue water near the middle of the lake. He wrapped the two trout he caught in brown paper and cooked them over hot stones while we sat shoulder to shoulder, watching concentric ripples flatten themselves after I tossed in pebbles. We finished the white meat that fell apart at the touch of a fork, while cornbread spilled butter over our fingers. I leaned my head against the scratchy wool of his sweater.

"Willie, why did so many crazy things have to happen? So much dying. First my father, then Claudia. I can't remember much about Daddy alive, only the shape of a horrible gray coffin."

"I'll remember him for you, Cady. He was the finest man I've ever known. If it wasn't for him I'd still be doing some kind of work in a mill eight hours a day. I think that's why I chose to be a landscape architect--to be free of a building, making live things break out of the earth."

"He would be so disappointed in his children."

"Not you."

"Did I tell you Emory is stationed on Guam in the Pacific? And surrounded by the natives for company? He should feel right at home."

He laughed. "He'll do fine."

"But Claudia. Such a terrible waste."

"Yes, but, Cady, I saw things in Iraq that are beyond any words you or I even know."

The sun dropped behind the tree line on top of the mountains and shafts of red light lay along thick gold foliage. A loon flew over our heads and called out to us.

"Let's try to even it up a little." He pushed me flat on the blanket.

"Even what up?"

"All the misery each of us has known. Let's do something very beautiful."

"Like this?"

His startling blue eyes blazed down at me. Sometimes Willie did not answer questions with words.

# CHAPTER 24

Before Thanksgiving Miss Eugenie handed me her Christmas list. My breath stopped for a moment. Walking up and down the decorated aisles in stores on Cherry Street had been her one outing of each year, shopping for each child living in the Pleasant Grove Orphanage for Colored Children. She had taken me with her as a young child to help choose gifts for the girls; Emory gave his advice for the boys, usually sports equipment. Making a good Christmas for the children had been my father's pet project; after his death it became one of the few leaks in the dike of seclusion Miss Eugenie chose for herself through the years. I turned aside to dam the rush of tears.

"Maybe Dola would rather have cash this year." I said.

"No. She likes to open the paper and ribbons. And ask about Eula Belle's dress size. And don't forget Eula Belle's daughter."

Glancing down the list I would not let myself tell her Emory would not need a cashmere sweater on Guam.

I bought a small tree for the console table in the entrance hall and decorated it blindly.

"It's pretty, baby," Dola said when I finished.

"Is it?" I looked straight into her eyes. "I really want it to be because . . ."

"Don't say it," she put one hand over my mouth. "Don't say nothing more."

Pearsons Drug Store made frequent deliveries now with pain medication for Miss Eugenie. Dr. Parker happened to be in the neighborhood four or five times a week to climb the stairs for a visit with her.

Late one January afternoon as I walked him to the front door, I said, "Give me enough time to get Emory here from Guam."

"Miss Cady," he shifted his hat from one hand to the other. "I think it would cheer Miss Eugenie no end to have Emory pay a visit just about anytime now."

After he left, Dola told me to call.

"It's Miss Eugenie," I said to Emory.

"Go on. Tell me," he said.

"It's bad, Emory. Come home."

"I'll get the first trans-Pacific flight going anywhere and then fly into Warner Robbins."

"Hurry."


I'm sure he did. But while Guam time was blending from the gold and blue of a mid-Pacific afternoon to deep purple night over San Francisco, opening the sky to a hazy yellow noon over Macon, time had slowed to one final minute for Miss Eugenie. It's strange about time. It rushes, drags, skips along, until suddenly on a whim, it stops.

The impressive rites of the Roman Catholic Church started Miss Eugenie on her journey with Father Deleraux and Sister Acquin beside her. Dola and I held hands at the foot of her bed at dawn. To everyone's disappointment but hers and mine, it was not angels and saints she welcomed in her last moment. She lifted one hand languidly from her bed and reached into early morning shine. "Sam," she said.

At the kitchen table in late afternoon, Dola blew her nose into a paper towel. "Ain't go' be no more crying now--she where she done always want to be." She wiped her eyes. "But it going to be lonely 'round here without all those folks in them black clothes. We was beginning to be good friends."

After Emory arrived and went upstairs to his old room for the evening, and while Sambeau slept, Dola and I sat shivering on the back porch steps.

"I wish I could have known her better," I said while she patted my hand.

"You talking crazy. You is just like her."

"No, no. I never understood her or knew what really made her tick. She was a very private person, Dola, I know that much."

"Not so damn private. She had two big loves in her life-- your daddy and what she was. And you is the same.

You love that Willie Fosters and you love what you is, it being a little different from what <u>she</u> was, but not that much."

"I wish I understood what you're saying," I put my head down on my knees.

"Someday you will, baby." She patted my head.

Emory, Dola, Maybelle and I stood at Redcliff with Miss Pridey Buckingham and the Hollingsworths; Daddy's two brothers with their wives wrapped in mink against winter wind were across from us at the private grave-side services. As we left the family plot in the cemetery I saw Willie standing beside a large monument on the graveled road leading down to the Confederate graves. Dola's hand on my arm restrained me from running to him.

Miss Eugenie's will was read by Harrison Carcy, Esquire, in my father's study with Emory and me facing the clear polished desk cluttered with dust of memories. Mother bequeathed all stocks, bonds, our small interest in the Worthington firm, all monies in Citizen and Southern National Bank to Emory. The house on the two acres bordered by Vineville and Bentley Avenues was left in the otherwise empty hands of her surviving daughter, Cady, and to her grandson, Samuel Beauregard Sorensen.

After a drink of brandy all around, Harrison left and I threw my car keys to Emory. "Go celebrate your inheritance in style. I'm really tired and I want to be alone."

I found Dola in the kitchen. "You are looking at a member of the Nouveau Pauvre Society."

"What that be?"

"The newly poor," I explained the will to her.

"Your mama never paid no mind to money or cared nothing 'bout it. Miss Genie loved this place. Her roots was deep here -- her life with your daddy and bringing up her chirrun on this place. She know'd you would step on it soft-like."

"She was right. I won't be able to afford any shoes."


I stood with Emory before the mantel in the living room having sherry while we waited for the taxi which would take him to the first leg of his flight back to Guam.

"Will you come back?" I asked him.

"Cady, we'll always come back, you and I, whether we want to or not. Our blood is here. It will never let us go lightly. But I have a freedom in the Navy I don't feel in the South anymore. Too much of what our family had is gone. I don't like elephant graveyards. No more pouring over old ivory bones for me. And there's a woman in Honolulu, a few years older than I am-- divorced with two children. We understand each other. Accept each other."

I walked to the taxi with him. "No bag of fried chicken and watermelon pickles to throw away once you've turned the corner," I squeezed his arm.

He looked startled. "I always gave Dola's lunches to the cab driver. How did you know?"

"Come back when you can bring your new family." I kissed his cheek. "To peace, Emory."

"When is it safe to come by the house?" Willie asked on the telephone from his motel room on the outskirts of Macon later that night.

"It depends on what you mean by 'safe'. Would people talk if they knew about us or saw us together? You can bet on it. Would you be safe from my terrible need for you this very minute? No. Never."

"Leave the back door unlocked. I'm on my way."

# CHAPTER 25

Dola and I sat on the back porch steps after breakfast on a magnificent October morning. Fisher had come down from Forsythe to be with us two years earlier, and now we watched him again while he raked fallen oak leaves in slow motion, stopping often to lean on the rake handle and smell the air. He told us he felt its changes settle around him and perk up his skin. Daniel lay at the back door, his head on his paws. My heart leapt high in my throat the first time I saw him stretched in the circle of sunlight that had been the waiting-place for my Follow, but now I welcomed Daniel filling the long-empty spot.

The edition of The Macon Telegraph I held announced another container strike in San Francisco and Los Angeles.

"Do you hear that grinding noise?" I asked Dola.

"I don't hear nothing but the Vineville School bell ringing and I hopes Sambeau done made it on time."

"No," I said. "Listen closely and you will hear the mills of the gods cranking up."

"I don't know nothing 'bout no kind of mills but cotton mills and they is cranking down, I hear tell."

"The mills of the gods grind exceedingly fine,"I said.

"If you ain't going to talk sense I go get to my dishwashing."

"Stay," I reached to hold her arm. "I need you. Sambeau's father is in a business that will be affected by the strike on the West Coast."

I showed her the newspaper picture of dockworkers' placards held high in the air with large letters spelling "STRIKE".

"Now ain't that just too bad."

Eric's letter came a month later without Sambeau's support check. The Sorensens had been forced to sell the ranch in Pebble Beach and were barely able to meet expenses of the staff and maintenance of the Vallejo Street house. Everything was pouring out, nothing in. They were desperate. He, Buffie, and little Eric felt the pinch terribly with Buffie actually doing her own housework. "This miserable strike has our very lives tied up and we are really being squeezed," he had said. Under the circumstances the support checks were impossible and if I wished to contest this decision, contact the law firm of . . . Then he sent his regards to all the lazy Southerners--those who had been born to ease and had always taken it for granted while watching it slip away due to their incredible lack of ambition for the really important things in life.

I laid the letter on the table. "Hard times are upon us, my friend. I'll have to get a job."

"Hoo! Sweet Lord in the skies."

After a minute I said, "We could rent out rooms."

"That ain't lady-like."

"It's more lady-like than standing on a street corner with a tin cup. But maybe I'll think of something."

Uncle Andrew called me to have lunch with him. "Considering your lack of education, Cady, the employment field is very narrow."

"Yes, well, I know I didn't finish college."

"From what I have observed, your conversion to the Roman church was not too permanent nor binding."

I lifted my coffee cup and stared across the table in the restaurant into his glacier blue eyes. "I guess I resist change," I said. "They seem to be going all out for it in Atlanta but down here in Macon time is steady and slow as the Ocmulgee."

He nodded. "I have spoken to the new rector at St. Matthew's who's willing to believe your few years as a Roman Catholic never happened. I told him you could type reasonably well and I hope that's true. You can handle his mail and appointments. The salary is small but the atmosphere will be pleasant and if it doesn't work out we'll find something else."

"Thank you, Uncle Andrew." He looked down at the floor rather than meet my eyes directly. We both knew he and his family were living in clover because of my mother's proud reluctance to fight him and his brother in court for our legal rights to the firm after Daddy's death. He had died without a will.

"Let's close off most of the upstairs," I told Dola that afternoon. "Seal off furnace vents and close the fireplaces. I'm not afraid to be here alone at night with Fisher and Daniel out in back."

"Don't count on Fisher. He acting strange and talking lots about his place up-country. Don't sound too good."

I called him in for coffee the next morning. "Don't leave us, Fisher. I can't pay you but I can keep a roof over your head and Dola's cooking isn't too bad. I'll try my best to take good care of you."

"Missy, it time for Daniel and me to go. I come on down here a spell ago to help out, but we gots to get on back home now."

That night for the first time in weeks I laid my head down on my dressing table and wept. I knew he and Daniel were going back to the house in the pine woods to sit in the rocking chair on his front porch and wait for death to walk softly through his small patch of corn, barely rattling the dry leaves so gently would it step.

I was awake long after midnight tiptoeing down the hall to see moonlight lying pale and cool on Sambeau's bed in Claudia's old room. At the window I saw that it lit the tattered branches of the Greenery. The spot where Willie and I had first awkwardly, beautifully kissed was shadowed by trunks of the trees and hidden from my sight. The high limb from which Claudia had taken flight jutted out against the autumn moon like a riderless broomstick. I felt rather than saw the mound where my Fellow lay buried. His grave was surrounded by stones from the old fish pond--beginnings and endings that I had learned to accept as the cycle of sun crossing over The Oaks to fall behind the chinaberry tree, come day, go day.

I walked back to my mother's bed and lay on it under her delicate white quilt, my fingers idling the brass crucifix that had stayed on her bedside table as long as I remembered.

As dawn moved across the sky and gentled the few leaves left on the largest of the oak trees outside Miss Eugenie's window, I slept.

# CHAPTER 26

William Fosters, Landscape Design, Inc. opened a branch office in Atlanta in February. On the super highway Willie could drive to Macon in a little more than an hour. I felt champagne flowing through my veins when I awoke every Friday morning knowing Willie would here by sundown.

"This will be a challenge," he said the first weekend. "Seasons here are different from Virginia, some shorter, some longer. By the way, Miss Pridey next door has asked me to restore her acre. Any suggestions?"

"Promise me you'll make it beautiful. I wish it could look like an extension of The Oaks but our flower beds are gone. They were Joe Henry's and Miss Eugenie's talent, not mine."

"I'll change that," he said, "starting next month."

"Just please leave the four o'clock bush by the back porch. I strung flowers from it on a pine straw every afternoon for my Daddy when he was dying. I wasn't allowed to see him but Dola took them in to him. He was in and out of consciousness but she told me he always reached for them."

"I'm sure he knew, darling," he said.

"Maybe. But please leave the bush where it is."


In early April we stood by one of the back windows waiting for the sun to push aside mist that lay on the grass like one of Miss Eugenie's white eyelet coverlets. Willie's workmen had sifted and churned the earth and I smelled it stirring. New plantings were taking their first timid look at The Oaks and I rushed to the windows each morning to make them feel welcome. I leaned back against Willie's chest.

"Once I read somewhere there are three things that can never be filled--the top of the sky, the stomach of a jackal and the eyes of man. Man can never see enough in his lifetime to satisfy him or fill him up."

Willie's hands moved the straps of my nightgown off my shoulders. It fell around my feet.

"I can't speak for a jackal," he said, "but I agree about man."

Later I asked him why he hadn't planted anything around The Greenery. "That surprises me," I said, lying with my head against his shoulder. "Surely calla lilies should be there or something white to remind us of how innocent we were then, as you may remember."

"I remember every second. But I like the plain green of kudzu. Green is the color of youth and beginnings. The color of the bounty of life begins with green. It did for me."

I held him against me. "I love you so much. Never leave me. Please God, never leave me."

Willie drove down in the middle of the week for his forty-ninth birthday. "Don't forget," I said when Dola brought his glowing cake into the dining room after dinner, "that I am five years younger than you."

"Amen." Dola helped him fill the dessert plates. "And a million years wiser than God or so she done told me many times."

"I had a good teacher. You. Stay and have a piece of cake with us."

She refused to sit at the table but stood leaning against the mantel while she finished her slice. "These store-boughten cakes ain't got it. I could'a made a better one."

"This one is fine and you do enough." I looked at her in the dim light of early evening. Her gray hair was cut short now at a beauty shop each month. The old plaited pomaded squares on her head were gone along with the ample breasts and stomach. Occasions for her special tea came less often, once a week at most.

Three days later she found me squatting by flower beds, looking at new shoots as if I were staring down through a Tiffany's counter.

"Eula Belle coming down Wednesday-next. It the spring holiday in high school."

"Great," I looked up. "It's been a long time, almost a year since I've seen her."

"Well, I'll make some kind of vegetable pie. She won't like my Easter ham now that she don't eat no meat or sugar. My only living kin had to go and take leave of her senses."

I heard gravel scatter in the drive at noon on Wednesday when Eula Belle's sea-blue Mustang sports car stopped at the front door. "You drive like Sambeau," I said as we held each other. "And designer jeans. You look great!" She had the flawless posture of many black women, her long neck held with the grace of a ballerina.

"How is Sambeau?" she asked. "I wish I had a fine-looking son somewhere in law school."

"He's spending Spring Break with his girl friend's family in North Carolina. And you have a fine looking-daughter in nurses training. Count your blessings."

A small frown grew between her eyes. "Yes, Ida will make a good nurse, I know that. She's majoring in home health care."

After her greeting with Dola, we stood on the back lawn where two of the trees reached for each other above our heads.

211

She looked up into the branches. "'Let there be spaces in your togetherness and let the wind dance between you. Kahlil Gibran. We read a lot together in that rickety old swing over there," she said. Suddenly I felt shivery as new leaves.

"Your mama's bookcases gave me a good start after we put aside our paper dolls. Remember when we used to build houses for them on these old roots?"

"Of course I do. I was always jealous of yours. No wonder you're an art teacher--you had such originality in everything."

She moved me toward the back lawn swing. "I'm an assistant principal now, Cady. In a mostly white school. Can you believe that?"

"Of course. I'm delighted for you."

She stopped. "Cady, you love this old place so much. You used to tell me those trees sang to you at night and only you could hear the words."


"It's true. They did. Each one is my friend. Miss Eugenie cut down three of them after Daddy died--who knows why my mother had such strange ideas--I still have five. The trees will always belong to me and they know it."

The shiveryness covered me again.

"Cady, could we sit down on the swing for awhile? I've been thinking about this a long time. Auntie is failing. I saw it today and I've seen it in the handwriting in her letters for months."

My stomach dropped. "We're all getting old, Eula Belle. You remember Willie Fosters--he's almost gray now."

She laughed softly. "Ever since I can remember you've loved that boy."

"Boy! He's in his forties."

"It comes and goes so fast like sun crossing the sky. But that's what I'm trying to explain, Cady. I want Auntie to come with me to Hapeville. She's tired and I want to take her back to my house."

"But you work, Eula Belle. She'd be lonely while you're away at school." My eyes stung. "And it's cold in Hapeville. Her arthritis would be worse."

"We'll take good care of her, Cady. And Hapeville is only an hour away on the interstate. You could visit anytime."

"This is her home, Eula Belle." I leaned forward. "Since she's lived in my old playhouse I've put in a reverse-cycle air-conditioner and everything I could think of to please her. It's been hard on my salary from the Church but I've tried to take good care of her."

We sat frozen. Willie's jonquils stood motionless, listening.

"Cady, you are unique in your love of `place'. I think it's because--well, your family was unusual. If Mr. Sam had lived there would have been more closeness, stronger bonds between you and your kin. But you missed that, Cady. You poured yourself out on this land here. I'm Dola's `people' and she's mine."

"She's been with me ever since I was born, Eula Belle. You know that." I leaned back and closed my eyes. "But I can't keep her if she wants to go."

"She doesn't want to go, but she should anyway. I'm her blood. I'm her race. I want to let her slip away feeling she's somebody on her own, not with a life sentence of being a `house darky' behind her."

I jumped up and faced the swing. "How dare you speak to me that way! Dola has never been thought of as a 'house darky' for one minute of her life here. Not one. I am insulted for myself and for my mother."

Eula Belle stood and put her arms around my stiff shoulders.

"You can't possibly understand, Cady, because you're white. Facts are facts. She's a colored cook now and always has been-- someone who's worked for many years in your kitchen. No matter how pleasant you all made it for her, she's been your servant, coming and going through the back door and that's a fact. For the rest of her life, she should be a woman who lives with her own people and knows the richness of <u>that</u>."

"Damn you, Eula Belle, damn you!"

"Oh, Cady," we held each other.

"Life is shit," I said finally. "Dola told me that once long ago and she was right."

"Cady, Cady, you'll never change. Never." She pulled back a little and looked at me. "We'll keep in touch, you'll see."

"In a pig's eye!"

She laughed. "I can tell you've been very much under the influence of my Auntie."

"You bet your sweet ass I have," I said, blowing my nose.


We walked slowly down the driveway with our arms around each other's waists. She took a package wrapped in brown paper from her car and handed it to me. "These are Tibetan prayer flags. Tie them to your precious trees in back and everytime one moves in the wind God will read the prayer it's saying."

I opened the package and held it. "They're beautiful. You've been almost around the world, Eula Belle, and you keep coming back to Georgia. There must be some bad memories here for you."

We faced The Greenery when we reached the car. "Listen who's talking," she said. "When you find out the answer let me know, you hear?"

"Give me a few more weeks with Dola. I'll pack for her. Miss Eugenie's closets have never been touched and there may be some things in there she'd like to have. They were best friends, you know."

"I know. You all have always been quality folk."

I pinched her slender arm. "Don't give me any 'Aunt Jemima' talk, toots. I know you too well."

She laughed. "It's good to know you'll never change, Cady. And we'll really see more of each other now than ever before."

I knew she was lying. After the Mustang melted into the flow of traffic headed north on Vineville Avenue, I allowed myself the luxury of tears falling unchecked.

# CHAPTER 27

Eric's letter lay beside me on the back lawn swing. I turned away from it and looked up into the secrets of the trees. How many people had these oaks hovered over through life, and given life beyond life--Indians, British settlers, then the splurge of the land with early planters and black slaves, the tragic time that could never be understood except by those who lived it. The deep gullies of my life had dead ends that somehow circled back to the oak trees and red clay waiting to welcome me with their unfailing composure.

When I was five Emory and Claudia had told me why the soil of Georgia was red--the flat lands, roads, banks, hillsides that grew up into mountains. Confederate blood, they said, that was spilled to keep our land intact, had soaked into the ground that still flaunted it with such love and pride it would never fade. During the winter of my third grade in grammar school, a teacher from Illinois explained to the class that dirt of the southern region of the United States held an excess of iron which caused its rust color. I felt relieved and lightened--it belonged uniquely to us whatever the reason for its color.

Watching the chiaroscuro of leaves above me, I knew Eric aimed the words of his letter at my Southerness like a sheath full of arrows. I rested my head on the back of the swing to let the two-note whine of the chains lull my senses. I felt hands from a long-ago past meet around my throat, threatening again.

I lifted the letter. Eric's family had been leveled. That bastard strike wiped them out completely, unalterably, helped by unlucky investments they had made. They resigned years ago from the Athletic Club, the San Francisco Yacht Club; he, Buffie and young Eric now lived in a rat-hole near a commercial district with a lousy view of a small back yard with two scrounge bushes in it. His parents had the small quest house on Gwendolyn and Doug's new place in Palo Alto (thank goodness Doug's practice was flourishing due mainly to his "talent" with women patients). Life was a real bitch but his mother was hit the hardest of them all. The strain of their financial collapse had caused her to have paroxysms of asthma that threatened her life, really ruined it with all the suffering involved in one of her attacks. Medical bills were incredible in spite of Doug's help. Nels and Gladys were old now, beaten by a fate over which they had no control. Under the circumstances, he felt their grandson (and his lawyers were well aware of Sambeau's trust in The Oaks) would wish to help them ease their last years on earth a little. Sambeau bore their name and their blood (so important to crazy Southerners) and it was a moral obligation he was certain his son would agree to. The side acreage of The Oaks was useless land to us, but would sell--his law firm had investigated--for a good price considering its location. Of course, when and if his job distributing paint and building supplies got into high gear, he would attempt to repay the estate at an interest rate of four percent.

Behind my closed eyelids I felt late afternoon sun move through the leaves, from light to dark and back to light again with the rhythm of the swing. A patch of shade lingered. Dola looked down at me.

"I known you too long not to tell something's troubling you bad. I could set your supper up out here. We ain't having much."

"Won't you please sit down? I'd really like to be with you," I said.

She brought out a tray with a pot of tea and a bottle of rum, then lowered herself with a heavy plop into a lawn chair.

The strong hot drink eased its path inside me, relaxing muscles I had tightened without knowing it.

"I just ain't got one word in my head to say," Dola read Eric's letter and leaned back in her seat. "Except that I can see clear that it's flitting through your mind right now to be a goddam fool."

"Don't, please, Dola."

"I going in the house in a minute and call up your uncles. They is money-mad theirselves and they just might can talk some sense into you. And Miss Aggie, too. She always been a pain in my behind but she ain't nobody's fool. Like you is."

"Don't trouble yourself. The buck stops here with me."

"You ain't right in your head."

"Don't use that word."

"What word?"

"Right. Or wrong. They're relative. I mean, what is, is."

Sunset cicadas throbbed in my ears. I would lose three oak trees, not the important ones in The Greenery, but three old dear friends from the beginning of my memory. Maybe the new owners of the land would find a way to build around them.

Repay the money? Could Eric give me back a piece of my soul?

My hangover woke me the next morning; I walked down to the kitchen carefully.

"Dola, please don't slam the pans down so hard. My brains pound with every sound."

"You ain't got no brains."

"Well, whatever is in the top part of my head hurts terribly."

"Justice is mine, say the Lord."

"The Lord said a lot of things, Dola."

"Tell me one thing He say 'bout common sense. That I'd like to hear. You give up half this place belong to your family more years than I can count. It should go down to your son, his son, and then on and on. You give it up to that old devil-woman that treat you so mean and hateful."

Willie called from his Richmond office two days later.

"Please tell me that you of all people understand," I said. "Once, just this once, I have a chance to pay something back. My family, Miss Eugenie's family especially, always took so much for granted--their due, their worth. I can change things a little now, turn the tide for the first time in our history. You understand that, don't you? Please say `yes'."

"I won't ever lie to you, darling. I won't tell you how I feel about it. Maybe later, but not now."

"Willie, I need you so much."

"Cady, this has to be your decision alone."

<u>Alone</u>. Nobody understood. It wasn't our land I was giving away. It was our damnable pride.

I received a good price for the acreage all the way from the far side of the wrought-iron gate down to the end of the block at Bentley Avenue. The driveway leading to the back of the house stayed with us.

Harrison Carey, Esquire, mailed a sizable check to Eric who acknowledged it by signing and returning the green card that was sent with the certified letter.

Three months later, Sambeau, home for Thanksgiving from Vanderbilt University, watched with his friends while a bulldozer ripped up grass and shrubbery for the Neo-Grecian Medical Arts building that was due to rise in their place.

I saw him put his foot up on the lowest plank of the ladder Emory had nailed to the trunk of the biggest tree in The Greenery long ago. Claudia had made a one-way trip up the same steps.

"Stop!" I called out to him.

I felt Dola's hand on my arm. "Hush," she said. "Quiet yourself. If you done gone this far with the old times don't chicken out now and be half-ass. Close that door tight and let it be."

# CHAPTER 28

Eula belle called to say she would pick up Dola around noon on Saturday-next so be ready. On Friday after the packing was finished Dola gave me her last instructions.

"This here is what's called a stove, this here is the sink, the ice box and the toaster. If you forgets how to boil water ask Zeldee next door to help you. If worse come to worse call me up in Hapeville."

"I just might surprise you, oh wise one. Maybe I'll have you all down here for a five course Thanksgiving dinner next year."

"Hoo! Five course. That be peanut butter sandwiches, store boughten ice cream and three cups of special tea."

"And what's wrong with that?"

Talking kept us going until sunlight touched the trees in places that told me it was the middle of the afternoon. The pale yellow November day had a gentleness that circled around me like butterflies.

I leaned against the back porch railing and looked over the lawn. Alone. This is my garden of olives and there will be not one soul to watch it with me.


"Dola," I turned to the kitchen door. "Let's have a party out here. It's still warm in the sun and we can have a very special tea party. We'll call it the Menopause Fling."

"I always knowed you was crazy."

"We're each facing a change in our lives, in fact, I'm facing two, so let's make it a good one."

"I reckon now you is making sense."

We sat in lawn chairs with a blanket around Dola's knees in case an afternoon breeze came up.

"Isn't Willie's garden lovely? I've weeded it every week and the asters have lasted a long time this year. And the chrysanthemums. Soon the holly bushes will spill over with berries."

"Baby." She touched my arm. "You is still a beautiful looking woman. Don't worry 'bout no opening of the flowers. Open yourself up. You owe it to the rest of them. all the rest of them."

I looked at her blankly.

"You owe it to the rest of this family to have a good life for yourself now. Push everything you got into every day and it would even things up for them all. Big and little bitty."

Little bitty? Her strange words floated past me like traffic sounds from Vineville Avenue. We sat quietly on lawn chairs listening to a dog bark a block away, a jet streak across the sky.

"Remember when the mill whistle used to blow three times a day?" I said. "Morning, noon, and quitting time. I loved that old sound. And the smokestack at the mill always gave us weather predictions. If the smoke didn't go straight up in the air it meant rain was coming."

"Yeah. I remember."

"Are you warm enough?" I asked. "Have some more tea."

"I reckon I will. My tea parties is done run dry when I leave here. Eula Belle ain't going to take to no rum bottles, I can tell you that."

"I'll make a deal with you. I'll try to be happy if you will. At least let's give it a hell of a try."

We touched cup rims.

"Amen," she said.

She dozed a little, then sat up with a start. "Oh Lord." She lay back. "I forgot. I ain't got to fix no supper."

"No, my friend. Never again. I want you to let your days flow by you now like the Ocmulgee. Soft and slow."

"We got a lot in common, that old river and me. We's the same color and almost the same age."

"Dola, do you remember when Willie was first missing and you told me about how hard it was to be black?"

"Yeah. I remember. And I told you how you gets used to things. Almost."

"Nothing's perfect anywhere," I said. "Except maybe my childhood here under these old trees."

After a few minutes she reached for my sweater sleeve. "Oh, baby. It wasn't nowhere near perfect. Not even good. Some of it was bad, real bad."

I sat up and looked at her lying back with her eyes closed. "I remember the terrible sadness when my Daddy died," I said. "It hung over everything like California fog but it lifted after awhile. Miss Eugenie never recovered but life went on for the rest of us. Eula Belle and I played out here under these trees, Emory had his horse and probably a lady-love somewhere, I think, and Claudia--well, I guess that's something I'll just never understand."

Dola sat with her eyes closed.

"All my life," I said, "I've wondered if someway maybe I could have changed it. I knew she loved Willie." I sipped heavily from the hot rum cup. "I would have given him up, left here, done anything if I could have kept Claudia alive. It will haunt me all the rest of my days. Wondering."

"Baby, it was nothing you could'a changed. Ease your mind on that. There is some should look back and wonder but you ain't one of them."

"Then who?"

She lay back in the chair. Her hands circled the tea cup, lifted it to smell its richness, then took another sip. Still with her eyes closed, she shook her head. "Maybe I ain't got no right to take this alone to my grave. I wouldn't rest easy if'n I thought you was carrying that burden heavy-like."

We sat on the porch while the sun moved slowly down to the chinaberry tree. Even the cicadas faded until suddenly their song was still.

# CHAPTER 29

"If it hadn't been for you two girls I'd been gone from this place long ago, up to live with my sister and Eula Belle in Hapeville. I couldn't leave you all and Mr. Sam would 'spect me to stay, take care of things. Seemed like nobody else gave a sweet goddam. Miss Genie was flitty like a piece of cloud and didn't care 'bout nobody but that Mr. Emory who did favor Mr. Sam, I say that much. He a good-looking man, good-looking since the day he was born.

"Your mama hover over him in them days like a ladybird in nesting time, rub him down with olive oil after his bath 'til his skin glowed like silk. Maybelle took care of you girls when you was little bitty, but not Mr.

Emory. He the light of his mama's eyes since day one. Anything he want he got. Worst part be that in spite of all that fussing 'round, he wasn't never worth shit.

"Mr. Sam loved Miss Claudia most. Look like he done seen the lost part of that child from the beginning. He the finest man I ever knowed of in my life--never raise his voice or do nothing to hurt nobody, always funny, making folks laugh 'round this place. Mr. Sam spoil Miss Genie something fierce when he alive. I done seen the fire between them when they in the room together even when she acting so high-tone ladyish she think she hide it, fool the world into thinking you chirrun got brung by the stork. I know'd better. I seen them once.

"He come home for lunch one day and ask Joe Henry to fetch him a special wine from the cellar, tell him where to find it and say he can taste a little hisself if he want to. The older chirrun was in school and you playing on your swings in the backyard while Maybelle watching you.

"Mr. Sam and Miss Genie giggling and talking over the lunch table and I come in to clear some dishes and there he be, kneeling by her chair and kissing her and she into it as much as he was. When I come back, they done gone up the stairs to their room 'til way in the afternoon. Mr. Sam run all the stores in his family so he didn't have no care 'bout getting back to work and didn't never give no damn what his brothers say no how."

"Hoo! When he dead they pay him back for marrying Miss High and Mighty. They get back most of the money he leave by telling Miss Genie they buy her out and give her a good price. Then, wham bang, four months after Mr. Sam buried out at Redcliffs, them two brothers of his come by with the lawyer-man again and tell Miss Genie times is hard, that the stores were near bankruptcy, and if she don't give in to what they say, they all go under."

"She so crazy with grieving inside she say 'yes' and sign some papers right here in this house and pretty soon our lives is different. Joe Henry not 'round every day and Calvin who drive the car done gone and I ain't got but one soul, Maybelle, a child herself to help me out. Ain't no wonder my bones ached. I thank the Lord above I done found the cure."

"Well, it weren't no cure but it did ease me some. I keep them decanters on the sideboard full and I be queen of the cellar. Miss Genie didn't never go down there--say she hate spider webs and she didn't drink nothing nohow, some sherry once in awhile, but her share was sure took up by Mr. Emory and Miss Claudia. He the one water down the whiskey and brandy decanters 'til they pale as golden wine. He take a big swig, pour some water in the bottle, and go along off knowing don't nobody know the difference but me. Miss Claudia she come by, fill a glass and didn't know she drinking half water. Praise sweet Jesus for that. She so frail and thin she couldn't handle it full strength."

"Manys a time Miss Genie done found her on a couch 'fore noontime passed out cold like a dead fish. She say to me, 'Oh, Dola, please help me with Miss Claudia. She gots that terrible middle-ear trouble again and we has to help her up the stairs.'"

"Miss Claudia open them green eyes and say to her mama 'Don't touch me, bitch,' but Miss Genie make out she don't hear and say, 'Poor angel, poor little lamb, she got to be in her bed.'"

"She not only didn't see nothing, she didn't hear nothing. That's how come she didn't know nothing. So I stayed here, take care of you girls. You I didn't worry too much 'bout. You got sass and took care of yourself. You didn't need me like Miss Claudia.

"The real bad times come 'bout ever' six months, something like that. The worst one be when Willie Fosters come home, then leave again for the war in Iraq. Miss Claudia get herself real drunk, man-drunk, all that afternoon and Miss Genie call on me to help her.

"I tell Miss Genie I undress her and put her to bed 'cause I done seen the mark on her dress when I was lifting her up the stairs. I knowed it could be real trouble. Bad trouble.

"When I got her in the bed, I sit beside her awhile and she start to moan, 'Oh, help me.' She look at me out of eyes full of pain and I think 'God help us both. It done happen again.'"

"Funny thing. I thought it might be Willie Fosters, making eyes with both you girls.

"He come to us when Mr. Sam bought that horse, that mean bastard, and need somebody to take care of it. Willie be 'bout ten then. He work in the cotton mill near this place and done some work on Saturdays downtown at the store for Mr. Sam when you too little to remember. He thought he a fine boy and hired him to take care of Thunderclap, after he get home from school and 'fore he work the night shift at the mill. Willie turn out so good and fit in so fine, Mr. Sam take him on after school, make him quit the cotton mill. Willie always a good-looking boy with blue eyes look straight at you. He good to you, baby, carved you tiny dolls out of wood when you was little, tell you 'bout why he brush the horse and clean him off after a ride.

"Miss Claudia never cared nothing 'bout no horse but she set for hours in the breakfast room windows watching Willie, whether he be with you or by hisself. She never said nothing, but I seen her eyes when she looking at him and I knowed.

"Well, I didn't aim to judge nobody and if he could give her a little gladness, then let God's angels just turn their faces away. I knowed I had got to see her through another bad spell again."

"I mop her face with a wash cloth and settle her pillow. The night air damp and chilly so I close the windows and move over to the fireplace, see could I stir up some coals. Miss Claudia in a fitful sleep, thrashing and turning in pain while pieces of the little life inside her was pushed out bit by bit. I put heavy towels underneath her and I change them again, carried them in buckets to the cellar to wash in the morning 'fore Miss Genie could see them. Them spells only lasted six or seven days and didn't nobody know what they was but me. Miss Genie thought they the natural monthlies Miss Claudia done always had hard times with."

"When the towels was soaked through and had the big clots on them, I knowed the trouble near 'bout over and I take that bucket outside and pour it on the roots way under the camellia bush side of the front gate by the driveway. The blood always sink into the ground fast and I cover up the pieces of teeny little life with dirt."

"I go back to the kitchen to fix her a cup of sassafras tea, heavy with whiskey. There be steps on the front staircase. I know from the sound it be Mr. Emory coming in drunk. He home on leave again, 'fore he go back to his Base."

"I follow Mr. Emory up the stairs careful-like so the tea don't spill. He stop at the door to Miss Claudia's room and, soft like a floating feather, he push it open. I reach the door in time to see him lean over his sister, her hair spread out black on the pillow and the glow of coals lighting up her face."

"'No, Emory,' she moan. 'Please leave me alone. Please leave me forever alone.'"

"He make out to get on the bed beside her. I step into the room and close the door. My hands tremble so bad the tea be splashing and burning, but I step up to him and I say, "Get out of here, you son of a bitch. I kill you dead if you ever touch her again, so help me God. Ain't nothing to lose to nobody if you be dead, so I telling you now. I be sleeping on a cot in this room 'til you is gone and if I sees your shadow walk past this door, I stick a knife in your ribs 'fore you gets down the hall. If'n you don't believe me, try me once."

"He stand up but his eyes won't fix to stare me down. He stagger out of the room and the door close behind him. Forever."

# CHAPTER 30

The house on the corner across the street whose curved verandah and back garden once welcomed footsteps from Georgia's old history was being torn down. I stood with Miss Pridey Buckingham under the elms that lined Vineville Avenue watching its windows stare down at the intruders as contractors walked around marking on their clipboards.

"Thus Anne Boleyn was led to the block," I said to Miss Pridey.

"Oh, Cady, darling, I'm afraid to open my eyes and look out of the windows in the mornings when I wake up. Scared I'll see something different, something new that's been changed from what it used to be like around here."

Berkley Hollingsworth drove by us in his Ferrari. His parents' deaths had made him rich but he told everyone his two divorces and three children were draining him dry as a bone. He made a U-turn in the suddenly screeching traffic and swerved his car to a quiet idle by the sidewalk where we stood.

"Morning, Miss Pridey," he called out. "How you, Cady? I hear tell you're still screwing that old mill boy and I hear he's moved in lock, stock and barrel. That must be some barrel he has. This's been going on much too long. It's downright indecent."

I took Miss Pridey's fragile arm and turned our backs to him.

"Don't worry about change," I kept my voice and face calm. "The really important things will always be the same for us. We won't let anything happen to what we are."

"We're a dying breed, Cady." She joined the required tableau under the elms as skillfully as a member of a Tudor court scene.

Berkley gunned the motor and raised his voice. "I also hear tell there's heaps of little children in colored town

who look a lot like your brother, Miss Uppity-whatever-
your-foreign name is. If I ever feel like slumming I'll give
you a call." He revved his motor and zoomed off.

"My Zeldee made some lovely pound cake and we
have hot-house strawberries. Please come share them with
me." Miss Pridey squeezed my hand.

"Sounds wonderful but I'm expecting a phone call
from Sambeau today. There's a law office in Atlanta he
wants to join. It's an old firm that Miss Eugenie's father
and her brother respected highly."

"You remember them, Cady, you remember those
times of your grandfather always, you hear?"

"I was barely even born, Miss Pridey."


"You remember them anyway, that once they lived and
that you are a part of them. When you are as old as I am
you'll know time is something we just don't understand
at all. One hand of the clock points to a number and one
hand touches another and each one is telling the truth.
Remember a clock is a circle--it goes around and around.
That makes me feel better. You feel good too, now, you
hear?" Her feathery touch brushed my arm.

"I'll try. But I dread going into that empty house again."

"I know how much you must miss your Dola. She surely served you all long and well."

After I shut the front door I leaned back against it, trying not to hear the echo of its closing while Miss Pridey's voice washed over me. "Served you long and well"--an empty, meaningless epitaph but was there one that could ever hold the right words?

I called Hapeville.

"Hey, baby. Is you doing all right?"

"I've been better," I said. "I just saw Berkley Hollingsworth which didn't improve my day much. And I never knew this old house was so big and empty. It rattles when I sneeze."

"I got news will make you perky. Mr. Willie drive down and stop by here last night, brung me a big country ham from Atlanta already cooked. Say he's going down to be with you for a spell. Maybe I ruint his surprise but I wanted you to know."

"Thank you, oh wise one. My hair looks awful and I'll have to have it done. And"--I had to rush the next words--"don't forget to keep in touch."

After I hung up the telephone I held my face in my hands while the hall clock pounded out its message that impersonal, uncaring time was moving as steady and sure as the white sun across the sky.

The eight story condominium rose slowly across the street like a new island lifting its curious head above a tranquil old sea that lapped at its edges. The beige and pink sign on the front lawn stated that Beckwith Construction Company was responsible for its birth; in the lower left corner small black letters said William Fosters, Landscapes, Inc. would ease growing pains of the new life.

"I've seen the plans, of course," Willie said the next weekend. "They're going to have turrets on the corners of each four floors."

"Dear Lord in Heaven."

"And a moat around the whole building with a bridge that will be drawn up at night for safety."

"Help us, Lord."

He ruffled my hair. "I've talked them out of the turrets and moat. I'll do the best I can with a boxwood maze in front with flower beds at unexpected turns. The back garden I'll leave undisturbed but I'll have to reinforce the plants. Some of them are over a hundred and fifty years old."

"I'm afraid in time I'll forget what it was like before."

"Good. Nothing living stays the same, Cady. According to you that old house was alive and breathing but it had to change into something more practical."

"Your business is growth, Willie, putting in new life in place of old. I want things to stay as they were."

He stroked the back of my head lying against his shoulder. "My father was an old man when he was forty-five after working in cotton mills since he could remember. His brother died of black lung from coal mines in Kentucky. That house across the street belonged to a way of life my family never knew anything about. Your family was a part of it but it's gone now. The world of Miss Eugenie doesn't exist anymore."

"But it's lines were so clear and so fine."

"You didn't know how ugly some of them were." He shook my shoulders. "Open your hands, my love, and let it go."

We listened to the whine of bulldozers as they made another push against the inner frame of the house across the street.

I laughed. "I'm being held in the embrace of a naked man and I just said I was sorry the old ideals are gone."

"And with a mill boy at that. Someone who went to school when he was a little kid with a bowl haircut and cotton lint in his hair, cardboard in the bottom of his shoes, lying in Miss Eugenie Worthington's four-poster bed with her incredible daughter."

"Aging daughter."

"But terribly loved." He turned on his side toward me.

"Not so terribly, Willie. From my small range of experience I'd say it's terrific!"

# CHAPTER 31

"But you can't really learn from a cookbook. It's handed down by women of the family, generation to generation. I'd like to know of one d'Autremont woman who ever held a cooking spoon in her life."

"Well, I reckon you is speaking true. But forget the cooking. You got me to take care of you."

But I didn't. Now someone was taking care of Dola.

I decided on cold sliced beef with horseradish sauce, artichokes and a good Burgundy.

Willie put a red plaid blanket on ground moldy with dead leaves from another season. The Ocmulgee slid by us, bringing smells of treasure in the blue mountains to the north. A rhododendron branch that leaned too far over a bank somewhere floated by us, one soggy bloom riding on top. I toasted the day with a sip of wine as warm as blood, then it was gone. But nothing is really gone, I thought. The bottle of wine Willie and I drank on the brittle grass in Tennessee when he came back from Iraq could still warm me through every vein. I saw him standing on the shore, his beautiful young back arched to send the sinker flying to dark blue water in the middle of the lake.

The Ocmulgee was brown and bounced in places like a child at a party. I lay back on the blanket and watched the last of the sun deepen red wine in my glass.

"This is beautiful crystal," Willie said.

"It belonged to my grandmother."

"My grandmother drank spring water from a tin cup down a mountain trail in north Georgia."

The drum of cicadas invaded my head and I listened for a minute.

He lay beside me, hands cupped under his head. "We all live on a see-saw, like a cotton mill boy being offered a good government job. Like Georgia being brought to its knees on a whim of Sherman's and now its burned out city is one of the prizes of the South and with a population that's mostly black."

"How can you think of leaving our strong, gentle people and taking a job in Florida?"

"Miami's part of the see-saw I have to be in on. It will destroy itself or have a hell of a lesson to brag about."

"Which will it be?"

"I don't know but I want to tighten some of the rules. The Everglades is their last hold-out. I parked my car one night by a canal to watch." He leaned up and sipped his wine. "It was like crawling back through a time machine--as if the deer and alligators were looking around after the ocean had rolled back and uncovered ground for the first time."

The river slipped by us until it stumbled over a bare sweet gum root.

"And The Oaks?"

"Let Sambeau have The Oaks. You'll be a grandmother some day. Pass it down. That's what it expects."

"I can't. It's been the coming home-place of my entire life. More than forty years of letting oak trees shelter me."

"Shelter you from what? From living? That's what your mother did."

I sat up with my head on my knees, to hide my face.

"Don't split us up, Cady, for a couple of acres of land."

"There's a lot more here for me than land." I said. "You can't understand."

"Don't waste yourself, Cady, in dead history. We could be together where it's being made."

"I can only understand what I know about. My roots are what makes me <u>me</u>. I can't change that. I'm not sure I want to."

"I don't want you to change. But grow a little."


He lay on the blanket with his eyes closed. Wine slurred his voice. "The Everglades waits in the sun while Miami fights to find itself every day. The very old and the very new. Like Georgia."

His words clashed in my head. Mellow old centuries reached out for me. They had moved ahead with grace, curtsying to the inevitable.

I shook my head and drank another glass of wine. Too quickly. I felt fragile as the crystal. Willie pulled me down to lie beside him and bent over me. A low red bank separated us from the river that crept by, reluctant now to leave this particular beauty it was barely able to watch under the twilight sky. Willie performed the rich, warm, cherishing moves that had always told of our bonding. Could they now?

# CHAPTER 32

Summer has the longest days of the year and what I expected to be the shortest nights. They were both endless. Maybelle's daughter Noreen came in once a week to straighten the house. I welcomed her steady chatter about her fiancé who was in Afganistan. I listened, following her from room to room. Once her mother had suffered with me, a skinny young blonde, who wept with her head on the kitchen table when Willie Fosters first left years ago. I went to bed early hoping for the oblivion of sleep. After an hour I turned on the lamp and reached for a magazine. On the bottom shelf of the bedside table I saw the old Baltimore Catechism and opened it at random.

Question: What is a sacrament?

Answer: A sacrament is an outward sign instituted by God to give grace.

I turned my face in to my pillow and stretched my hand across the sheet to touch a wide space of emptiness.

Light summer rain tapped on the window. I opened my eyes and lifted my head. "Go ahead." I called out. "Water the damn weeds until they grow sky high."


Willie Fosters, I hope you enjoy saving your spicy saw grass and all those pretty alligators.

I opened the door the next day to Berkley Hollingsworth. "My cup runneth over," I said to him.

"Just thought you might like to drive out to a new place on the Cordele Highway that has great steaks."

"Come in, Berkley. I'm becoming a vegetarian but I can fix you a really nice salad."

After several glasses of Chablis I studied his face across the table. Flesh drooped with the weight of time like melting candles. His hair had faded to ash blond streaked with gray and his eyes looked bleary from too much drinking and too many years. "Cady, I'll never marry again," he twirled the stem of his glass. "Those rapacious women I married have picked me clean to the bone. But I can't see any reason on this earth why you and I can't provide each other with a little comfort. Especially since I've heard you've put that tacky mill hand out of your life at long last."

I reminded myself that Berkley was an invited guest in my home and made only a soft-spoken comment. "It surprises me a teeny bit to hear you, of all people, call anyone else 'rapacious', Berkley. That's kind of like comparing the Mississippi River to a little bitty stream bed. And I didn't put the tacky mill hand out of my life. He left me high and dry. As for providing comfort, I really don't need any right now. I've never been better." My smile at him across the table hurt my face.

When he followed me to the front door we shook hands.

"You still have a great-looking little ass, Cady," he said.

"Ah, Berkley." I reached to hug him. "I needed that. Come by again soon and we'll talk about the good old times."

"I can't remember any but we'll try to dredge up a stirs."

"Did you know we were pushed around in our baby carriages together?" I asked him.

"So I've heard. I wish I could remember seeing your diapers changed," he said.

I laughed for the first time in weeks.

Upstairs, the house--every room--ached for Willie. Rustles of the night were stirrings of longing. Fool. Lie here in your pineapple four-poster bed that saw your beginning and will probably hold your lonely, old lady bones withering in malignant stubbornness until the end, a disease that was fused in your genes. But what was the cure?

Ghosts of youthful spirits moved about the upper rooms. I heard the jingle of Fellow's collar.

At dawn I went outside and walked around the back lawn barefooted. Weeds were sprouting around Willie's azalea beds. I knelt to pull them out and held some of the soil from their roots in my hand for a minute. I lifted it to my face to smell the cycles of time that had melted into dust that dribbled away through my fingers--gray dust that slipped down into more gray dust. I leaned back on my heels and stared into azaleas gone to seed.

Had I been spending my cycles of time listening to an echo of a long-silent faraway place, a sensuous murmur that existed in my ears alone? Could the words be honest and true sifted through the relics of years or were they merely whispers of a drum roll, faint as the sigh of air moving across the grass with the rising sun. The echo dimmed and faded as gray dust settled around me.

In the middle of the morning I called long distance to Dola. "I just wanted you to know I'm sitting at the kitchen table thinking of you and having some special tea. Very special tea."

"Ain't it a little early for that?"

"I was thinking it was a little bit late. Dola, I'm leaving The Oaks. I have to go to Florida to be with Willie however he wants it."

Her voice was faint over the telephone. "That ain't no news to me."

"I'm going to do it fast because I can't fight anymore. I'm too tired to keep pulling against the tide." The paper towel was soggy in my hand.

"I don't know 'bout no tide, but I seen this coming for a long time, steady and sure like a sunflower."

"I really wish you were here, Dola. Is everything all right with you? Do you need anything?"

I heard a deep sigh. "I need to be setting there at that table right now with you. Else wise, I'm fine. You go on down to Florida, baby, and you be happy, you hear? Just don't send me no oranges. They gives me the runs."

Sambeau was hard to reach on the telephone. When he returned my call I said, "I have news for you and Judith presented on the most cherished of rare silver platters. I'm going to move to Florida to be with Willie."

"Great. Terrific."

"I know you'll take care of it and love it."

"Love what?"

"The Oaks."

"Sell The Oaks, Mother."

"Sell?"

"Judith and I are settled up here in Atlanta. The city is like crazy. We're part of it and we can't leave."

Sell The Oaks? "You were born here, Sambeau. You'd feel it creeping into your skin every morning when you opened your eyes. It's right here beside you whenever you take a step."

He laughed. "My last name is Sorensen, Mother. I'm half Yankee. My other grandparents were immigrants, remember? Sell the old place. Take the money and run. Do you want my firm to handle things for you?"

"Good Lord, no. My own flesh and blood selling this land. Uncle Andrew can handle it."

"Uncle Andrew is your own flesh and blood."

"Not by choice. And I'm not sure Uncle Andrew has any blood."

"Mother, are you having a few?"

"You are a Yankee! Down here we call it a 'gracious plenty'. Yes, I'm having a gracious plenty and I'll have plenty more after that. With grace. The first grace I've given myself in a long time."

"Just don't climb the stairs."

"I'm down at the kitchen table. It was the Delphic Oracle for you in your younger days where you heard all the wisdom this world has to offer."

"Don't cry, Mother."

"I'm not crying. If you'll feel better about it I'll go lie down on the living room couch now, the one that has three good legs, and let it wobble me to sleep."

"I'll call you in a couple of hours. Let me know when you plan to leave Macon. Judith and I'll come down lock up the house and all."

"No. Please, that's something I don't want anybody else to do but me."

Later I walked up the stairs to Miss Eugenie's bed and fell across it. Outside, sunlight lay in small patches on the roof of the playhouse, dallying with the shingles before sliding off to hide behind the chinaberry tree. I listened to sunset stirring of the leaves while they settled into dusk and waited for the heavy song of night.

"I'm going to leave you," I told them. "I never thought I could do it but this time I mean it."

Printed in the United States
38585LVS00001B/133-147